BEAU

BAYOU BROTHERHOOD PROTECTORS
BOOK FOUR

ELLE JAMES

*Sydney
Enjoy Elle James*

TWISTED PAGE INC

ISBN EBOOK: 978-1-62695-522-6

ISBN PRINT: 978-1-62695-523-3

Dedicated to Bandit and Charli, my sweet pups and sidekicks. Thank you for your unconditional love and for getting me out of my chair fifty times a day when I'm in deadline hell.

Elle James

AUTHOR'S NOTE

Enjoy other military books by Elle James

Bayou Brotherhood Protectors
Remy (#1)
Gerard (#2)
Lucas (#3)
Beau (#4)
Rafael (#5)
Valentin (#6)
Landry (#7)
Simon (#8)
Maurice (#9)
Jacques (#10)

Visit ellejames.com for more titles and release dates
Join her newsletter at
https://ellejames.com/contact/

BEAU

BAYOU BROTHERHOOD PROTECTORS
BOOK #4

New York Times & USA Today
Bestselling Author

ELLE JAMES

BEAU

CHAPTER 1

BEAU BOYETTE PULLED into the parking lot at the Gautreaux Chateau on the bayou west of New Orleans, Louisiana. Dressed in a Robin Hood costume, complete with a green coat, a quiver of arrows, a thick belt and the signature green hat, he felt ridiculous, mostly because of the goddamn green tights. He prayed his Brotherhood Protectors teammates hadn't seen him leaving the boarding house in Bayou Mambaloa. He'd never hear the end of it.

He dug into his jacket pocket for his cell phone. Having put off this call as long as he could, he needed to get it over with and clear his slate for however long his mission might take.

"Beau, *cher*," his mother, Josephine Boyette, answered on the first ring in her heavy Cajun accent. "*Comment ça se plume?*" Translated: How's it plucking?

Beau grinned at his mother's favorite Cajun saying. "*Bien, Maman.*"

"Why we have non seen you in da past week? You're gonna be here for da Sunday dinner, *oui*? It will be da first time in eight years since all ten of *mes enfants* have been together."

"*Maman*, I can't make the family dinner on Sunday. I got my first assignment and have to work."

"You no can put it off 'til Monday?" she asked.

"No, *Maman*," he said. "I work 24/7."

"You no in *l'armee* anymore. You come to da dinner."

"No, *Maman*. I'm not in the Army anymore, but I work providing protection for people," he explained for the fifth time since hiring on with the Brotherhood Protectors.

"Surely, you get a day off," his mother said. "Do I need to talk to da boss?"

God forbid his mother should talk to his lead over the Bayou Brotherhood Protectors. He'd never hear the end of the ribbing he'd get from Remy Montagne or the rest of the team. Or she could make it worse and take her complaint to Hank Patterson, the man who'd started the original Brotherhood Protectors organization.

Beau sighed. "*Maman*, you don't need to talk to my boss. I signed on to dis job, knowing it could mean working 24/7 to protect our clients. I'm just calling to let you know I won't be at da family dinner. I'll try to make it another time."

"But—" his mother started.

"*Je suis désolé*," Beau said. I'm sorry. "I have to go. My job starts tonight. *Je t'aime. Au revoir.*" He ended the call before his mother could get all wound up and talk for another thirty minutes.

Beau didn't have time to talk. He'd been hired by Senator Marcus Anderson to protect his daughter Aurelie.

Miss Anderson had received a number of death threats over the past week since the senator had announced his reelection campaign. At the same time, Aurelie had stepped in to lead her father's philanthropic effort to preserve the bayou.

Since the senator would be campaigning across the state, he wouldn't have time to be with his daughter to guarantee her safety.

That would be Beau's responsibility.

The senator didn't want his daughter to know he'd hired a bodyguard. At least, not yet. He'd warned Beau that his daughter could be headstrong and extremely stubborn, a trait she'd inherited from her father.

Great. Beau wasn't thrilled with the idea of babysitting a spoiled little rich girl with a rebellious streak. He'd have to be on his toes at all times to make certain she didn't ghost him and land herself in trouble with no one around to help.

What she probably needed was a good old-fashioned spanking to get her attention. He'd almost asked the senator if that was a possibility but had thought better of it.

This was his first assignment with the Brotherhood Protectors. He wanted it to be a success and good advertisement for future gigs. Word of mouth was the best kind of marketing in the security business.

He pulled on the green cloth mask he'd acquired with the costume, thinking it appropriate for this undercover bodyguard job.

The event at the Gautreaux Chateau was a masquerade ball to raise money for the senator's reelection campaign. Only the very wealthy had purchased tickets at ten thousand dollars each.

Beau wouldn't be going to the event if the Senator hadn't given him a free ticket. He'd have been standing guard at the door or pacing the perimeter.

Ten-thousand-dollar tickets?

No way.

He had the money, but he had other plans for his savings—a place of his own with a house and five to ten acres of good land where he could raise a garden, a cow or two, and chickens. If it was on the bayou...even better. He'd always wanted a boat dock and access to fishing whenever he had a spare moment.

His mother had offered to give each of her children ten acres out of the one hundred and twenty acres that had been in their family for over two hundred years. So far, only two of her ten children had taken her up on that offer.

As much as Beau loved his mother, he couldn't see living that close. As it was, being in the same parish was almost too close. He was always running into those of his siblings who hadn't left Bayou Mambaloa to find employment in the bigger cities, like New Orleans or Baton Rouge.

No. He wanted to purchase his own property, preferably on the other side of the parish, with a little distance between them to discourage his mother from "dropping in" whenever she felt like it.

Oh, he loved his mother, but he also loved his privacy. As a widow with no husband to occupy her time, Josephine Boyette took her mothering to the extreme, trying to solve every problem for every one of her children instead of letting them figure it out on their own.

He'd limited his time with her since he'd been back, afraid she'd dig into his problems and find out he wasn't as okay as he'd led her to believe.

He'd been working through his issues with the therapist the VA hospital had assigned since he'd returned from his last mission with the Army Rangers.

As the sole survivor of a helicopter crash, he'd been so messed up he hadn't wanted to get out of bed for a month. That and the broken leg hadn't helped.

But that was in the past. He'd been through hundreds of hours of physical and mental therapy and was more than ready to get on with his life.

His teammates who'd perished in the crash couldn't get on with their lives, and they'd never know the wonderful trouble of being psychoanalyzed by their mothers.

How many times had he been told he was the lucky one?

And why didn't he feel lucky?

A weight threatened to settle on his chest, pushing out the air he'd been breathing.

Now was not the time to backslide into the black funk he'd clawed his way out of over six months ago.

Beau pushed open the door of his truck and dropped to the ground. He squared his shoulders and marched toward the entrance, careful not to limp on the leg that would never be the same.

He was determined to do his best to help the senator, make a good impression for the Bayou Brotherhood Protectors and keep Miss Anderson safe.

A man in a black suit stood guard at the door, checking IDs and tickets of each guest as they arrived.

Out of his element at such a formal function, Beau adjusted his Robin Hood hat. When the guard asked for his ID, he presented his military ID, his ten-thousand-dollar ticket and raised his mask briefly.

Beau entered the 18th-century mansion and was immediately struck by the opulent marble flooring and the double sweeping staircases on each side of the foyer, rising to the second level. A man dressed in a livery suit held out his hands. "May I take your... jacket...or quiver of arrows?"

"No, thank you," Beau said. "But perhaps you can tell me where I can find Senator Anderson."

"The senator is in the ballroom receiving line," the servant said and waved an arm toward the sound of music coming from a wide-open doorway.

Beau crossed the marble floor and entered a large ballroom crowded with people in a variety of costumes.

A man wearing an Abraham Lincoln outfit stood just inside the doorway, greeting guests as they entered.

Abraham Lincoln held out his hand. "Welcome to the Harlequins and Heartthrobs Masquerade Ball and reelection campaign fundraiser. Thank you for your support."

Beau gripped the man's hand. "I assume you're Senator Anderson," he said.

The man dressed as Abraham Lincoln smiled. "Your assumption is correct. And to whom do I have the pleasure of speaking?"

Beau dipped his head. "I'm Beau Boyette, an agent

of the Brotherhood Protectors. I was sent to help you with your situation."

The senator's smile faded, and his grip tightened on Beau's hand. "Thank you for coming so quickly."

Beau's glance swept the ballroom. "Is the object of your concern here tonight?"

The man with the Abraham Lincoln top hat and black jacket gave a brief nod. "She is."

Beau looked around the ballroom again. "Will you introduce me to her to get the ball rolling?"

Abraham shook his head. "My daughter is a strong-minded, independent woman. She won't be happy that I've hired somebody to protect her. For now, I'd rather let you acquaint yourself with her. If that doesn't work, I'll introduce you as a son of a friend of mine."

Beau nodded. "As you wish. At the very least, could you point her out to me?"

The senator glanced around the ballroom. "She's dressed as Amelia Earhart, in trousers, a dusty-brown jacket and goggles instead of a mask." The man shook his head. "I couldn't get her to wear a dress to save my life."

Beau's lips twitched. "She sounds like she has a mind of her own."

The senator chuckled. "That she does." He lifted his chin, indicating direction. "That's her dancing with my executive assistant. At least the ballroom dance lessons that I paid for weren't wasted. They would've looked better if she were wearing the ante-bellum dress I had commissioned for her."

The woman in the goggles waltzed past Beau in the arms of a man dressed as a swashbuckling pirate.

Now, that was a costume. Beau wished he'd had more time to find a better disguise than the Robin Hood one, which was the last decent choice at the costume shop in New Orleans.

He hadn't had time to go to a different costume shop, given that he'd only been notified of this mission around noon that day. His only other choice was a hairy Sasquatch costume.

Although, he was now beginning to wish he'd gone with Sasquatch. He felt very exposed wearing green tights, even though the jacket was long enough, just barely covering his ass.

"Good luck keeping up with her," the senator said.

Beau's lips pressed together as he watched the woman laugh out loud at something the pirate said. "I'll take it from here," he said, leaving the senator at his post receiving guests.

Beau wandered into the ballroom, his gaze on Amelia Earhart, a.k.a. Aurelie Anderson. He stopped at a table serving lemonade and what appeared to be mint juleps. He chose a lemonade and stood back, watching Miss Anderson dance around the room with the pirate. As he sipped the lemonade, he thought through the different scenarios where he could introduce himself.

The woman appeared relaxed, dancing and talking with the senator's executive assistant. Her movements appeared effortless, a testimony to the dance lessons her father had paid for her to take. An orchestra provided the music, playing various reimagined modern songs in an 18th-century style.

As the song came to a close, Miss Anderson and her partner slowed to stop. The pirate gave her a sweeping bow and then waved a hand toward the open bar.

Aurelie shook her head and said something Beau couldn't hear. Then, she walked away from the executive assistant. She ducked through a doorway and disappeared.

Beau set his glass down on an empty tray and hurried to follow. He left through the same door that she had and walked quickly down a hallway. He spotted her pushing through another doorway further down the corridor.

Though he hurried to catch up, he came to an abrupt halt in front of the swinging door with a placard indicating that the room inside was the ladies' restroom.

Since he couldn't follow her through that door, he walked further down the hall and stood in front of the men's room, waiting for Miss Anderson to emerge.

A few minutes later, the senator's daughter emerged from the bathroom.

When she looked in his direction, Beau pretended to be coming out of the men's room. She only gave him a cursory glance before she headed back to the ballroom, her shoulders back, head held high as if she were marching into battle.

Beau followed and found her standing against the wall, her foot tapping to the beat of the music. Beau crossed to the lemonade table, snagged two glasses of lemonade and walked back to where Miss Anderson stood half-hidden by a potted plant. He stopped next to her without looking at her, his gaze on the people dancing across the floor. Eventually, he held up the glass to her. "You look like you need this more than I do."

She took the glass from him and downed most of it in one long swallow. "Thanks, I did need that."

He chuckled. "Do you always dance so rigorously?"

She lifted her chin. "A wise person once told me to put your heart and soul into everything you do, or don't bother doing it at all."

"Have you ever bothered to do the nothing at all?" He quirked his lips upward on the corners in challenge.

"A number of times," the Anderson woman said.

"Now that you've consumed an entire glass of lemonade given to you by a complete stranger, did you stop to think I might have spiked that lemonade with a date rape drug?" he asked.

Her brow wrinkled. "You don't look like the type of man who would spike a girl's drink."

He looked down at his costume. "Is it the costume?"

She laughed. "Partly. And the fact that you wouldn't have given me the lemonade spiked with any drug with my father watching like a hawk." She lifted her chin toward the man dressed as Abraham Lincoln. "He's been watching me all evening. He even enlisted his executive assistant to have a pity-dance with me to keep me busy."

"I'm sure your father's assistant didn't consider dancing with you in any way pitiful." Beau tipped his head toward the couples dancing to the music. "You held your own on the dance floor."

Aurelie met his gaze. "You were watching that long?"

"I was," he admitted.

"That's kind of creepy," she commented. "I might reconsider my earlier opinion about you." She touched a hand to her throat. "Perhaps you did spike my lemonade."

Beau's lips twitched. "I didn't, but I can understand President Lincoln's concern for his daughter," he said. "Considering the fact he was assassinated, he has good reason to be a little paranoid."

Her lips curved into a smile, transforming her face and making it softer and more approachable.

"You have a point." She held out her hand. "I'm Amelia Earhart. Nice to meet you."

So, she was going to play it that way. "Robin Hood," he said as he took her hand.

Her grip was firm, not limp like many of the women with whom Beau had shaken hands.

"Robin Hood, you say?" Aurelie cocked an eyebrow in challenge. "I had pegged you as Peter Pan."

He released her hand and pressed his over his heart. "You wound me, madame." Beau shook his head. "I would think my quiver of arrows and the bow would have given it away."

She chuckled. "They are quite impressive. How about those tights? Should I assume anything about your sexuality?"

His hand remaining on his chest, Beau shook his head. "Again, you wound me, madame. I assure you I'm more attracted to Maid Marian than Friar Tuck."

Miss Anderson chuckled. "For what it's worth, the tights look good on you."

He dipped his head. "I'll take that as a compliment."

"As you should." She glanced around the room. "Now, if you'll excuse me, I'm working."

"Working?" he lifted both eyebrows.

Still looking around the room, she answered, "This is a fundraiser. My job is to make sure the guests are happy."

Beau nodded. "And happy guests mean more contributions to President Lincoln's reelection campaign, right?"

Her brow wrinkled. "Of course."

"Then, perhaps, you might consider entertaining this guest with a dance?"

Her lips twisted. "Sir, I believe you're quite capable of entertaining yourself." She started to walk away.

"Then perhaps, you might consider taking pity on a man in tights who is sure to be avoided by every available female in the ballroom and dance with me. I would consider it an honor," he performed a deep bow, "and a heroic way to help me salvage my eligible bachelor status."

She shook her head. "More likely salvaging your ego. Although, I doubt you'll lack a partner. Many of the matrons will be vying for you to join them in a dance."

"Only if I first prove I can dance."

Aurelie canted her head to one side, her gaze raking over him. "True. Not many men can dance. Or, truthfully, *like* to dance."

"I can and do like to dance. My mother made certain all her boys could represent the family properly on the dance floor."

"Forced to take lessons?" She shook her head. "Me, too."

"More like forced to learn." Beau hadn't always

appreciated having to learn to dance with his mother and sisters as his partners. Not until he'd grown older and interested in girls had he understood the value. The ladies usually loved to dance, and most of his male friends didn't or wouldn't. "My mother was a very good teacher. She and my father loved to dance at festivals and parties."

She drew in a deep breath and let it out. "In the spirit of showing the other women in attendance that you can and will dance, I suppose I could spare a pity dance with the man in green tights." She held out her hand. "Come on, Peter Pan. Let's show them what you've got."

"Robin Hood," he corrected as he took her hand and led her out into the middle of the ballroom as the orchestra began a new song.

After the first three notes, Beau recognized the song as "Can't Help Falling In Love," made famous by the late crooner Elvis Presley.

"Good grief," Aurelie murmured.

"It's a sign," Beau said as he glided across the floor, super glad his mother had insisted on him learning to waltz.

Aurelie needed little guidance to execute the dance. She usually had to lead when her male partners couldn't. With Peter Pan, she played a little push-me-pull-me until she finally let him take control. "You say your mother taught you to dance?"

He nodded. "She insisted on us learning to be as

fluid and graceful as Fred Astaire." Beau grinned. "She loved all his movies, especially those when he partnered with Ginger Rogers."

"Let me guess..." Aurelie said, "she made you watch the movies as well?"

He nodded.

"And your father had no say in the matter?"

"None," Beau said. "When it came to our education, both in school and on the dance floor, he let her take the lead."

"A hands-off father?" She snorted softly. "What's that like?"

"Oh, he wasn't a hands-off father; he just knew which battles to choose. He taught us other things."

"Like?" She prompted.

"How to open doors for women, the elderly, and...well, anyone." He grinned. "He taught all of us about the bayou, to include frog gigging, how to spot alligators, shrimping crabbing, fishing, cleaning and preparing the food we caught. He also taught us about vehicle maintenance like changing oil, tires and spark plugs."

"Even your sisters?" Aurelie asked.

Beau nodded. "Absolutely. Our mother could do all those things; she just preferred not to. Before all of us kids, she helped him on his fishing boat. Even after we came along, she still loved fishing with my father."

Aurelie frowned. "How many children did your mother and father have?"

"There are ten of us," Beau said and waited for the shock on her pretty face. He wasn't disappointed.

"Ten?" Her feet faltered.

Beau's arms tightened around her, and he effortlessly swung her out and back into his arms. "That's right. They had ten children."

"That's a lot of mouths to feed," Aurelie frowned. "Wow."

He laughed. "My grandparents considered my father an underachiever."

Her frown deepened. "Why?"

"His brother sired nineteen children. My father didn't even come close."

Aurelie's brow furrowed. "You're not serious, are you?"

"As serious as the heart attack that claimed my uncle's life when the youngest set of twins was only five years old," Beau said, his voice growing soft. He'd been in Iraq when his uncle had passed. His father had done his best to help the family out. Fortunately, his brother had been a shrewd investor and had taken out a sizable life insurance policy when he'd been younger. After selling the family boat-building business, his aunt had managed the investments and the houseful of children like the CEO of a major corporation.

"Youngest set of twins?" the woman in his arms asked.

"That's right," he said. "I think there are three or four sets of twins." Beau twirled her away and back into his arms. "Does that bother you that I'm from a family of many children?"

"No, why should it?"

"Do you even like children?" he asked.

She blinked. "Of course I do."

"Do you have any siblings?" he asked, though he already knew the answer.

Aurelie shook her head. "I always wished I had a brother or sister. You're fortunate to have some."

His lips twisted into a wry grin. "Others might not think so. There's never a moment's peace when we're all together."

"I hope to have children someday. Not just one child. I don't wish that on anyone. It can be very lonely."

"And quiet," Beau said with a sigh.

She laughed. "I take it you value silence."

"I do," he said. "But I love my brothers and sisters very much, even though they can drive me crazy at times."

The five-string quartet transitioned into another song, not a waltz, but one that allowed Beau to slow to a rocking motion. His arm circled the small of her back, and he pulled her closer. "Speaking of silence..."

He rested his cheek against her temple. "You smell good."

"What does that have to do with silence?" she asked, her body stiff.

"Nothing. But if we don't talk, we can almost imagine Elvis singing this one."

She moved in rhythm with him to the orchestra's version of "Love Me Tender."

Together, they fit perfectly, a fact that gave Beau pause. The more he held her, the more he wanted to.

Dangerous...dangerous thoughts.

Yet, he didn't relinquish his hold.

Slowly, her body melted into his. As the song came to its beautiful end, Beau dipped Aurelie low in his arms and kissed her.

As their lips met, the music ended.

She opened to him, letting him in for a brief and delicious taste. For a moment, their tongues touched and caressed. For a moment, he forgot where he was and that he was on a mission to protect this woman, not make out with her in front of her father and the rich and influential people there to contribute to the senator's campaign.

When he brought her back up, he stared into her goggles, wishing he could see her eyes. He wondered what color they were, what they would tell him and if she'd enjoyed the dance and the kiss as much as he had.

He might not be able to see her eyes, but he could

feel the change in her body where his hands still rested against her back.

Aurelie stiffened. "Excuse me."

She stepped backward, spun on her booted heels and darted for the hallway where the bathrooms were located.

Beau started to follow.

"What the hell was that?" a voice said behind him in a tight whisper.

He turned to face an angry Abe Lincoln.

"I introduced myself to your daughter." He couldn't have come up with a dumber response if he'd tried. But once it left his lips, he couldn't take it back.

"And that gives you leave to grope her on the dance floor? What kind of operation is this Brotherhood Protectors?"

Fuck.

He'd blown it with the man who'd hired him. What had he been thinking, kissing the man's daughter?

"My apologies, sir. It must have been the song." Beau glanced toward the hallway where Aurelie had gone. "If you'll excuse me, I need to follow her and make sure she's all right."

"Damn right, you do. And while you're at it, try not to molest her." As he turned away, he muttered, "What's wrong with the young people today?"

Beau didn't try to answer the man. He strode out

of the ballroom into the corridor. This time, he didn't see Aurelie walking into the bathroom. She was nowhere to be seen, as if she'd disappeared.

With the kiss still fresh on his lips, he ran to the ladies' room door and knocked on the contoured panel.

An older woman dressed as the Queen of Hearts pulled the door open.

Beau frowned. "Did you see Miss..." he thought better of asking if the woman had seen Miss Anderson and amended, "Amelia Earhart?"

The woman shook her head. "I was the only person in here." She stepped out of the bathroom, her gaze sweeping him from top to toe. "Let me know if you can't find her. I'm available all night." With a wink, she walked away.

Holy shit.

His first day on the job, and he'd already lost the client.

CHAPTER 2

AURELIE ANDERSON HAD NEVER BEEN KISSED in public, on a dance floor, with everyone and his brother in attendance, including her father.

She'd run from the ballroom out of embarrassment.

Or so she told herself.

If she were honest with herself, she'd call it what it was.

At lie.

She'd run from the ballroom...no... from him because that kiss—

Wow. Until that moment, she'd never known what it felt to have her world rocked by a single kiss.

Now. She. Did.

So, she'd done the only thing she could think of and ran.

For a woman who had control of every aspect of

her life, she'd just met a man who, in less than an hour, had made her lose control to the point she'd allowed him to kiss her in a public place with the most important donors in attendance who could potentially make or break her father's campaign for reelection.

In her bid to escape her wanton behavior, she'd aimed for the bathroom, but the Queen of Hearts had been there, applying bright red lipstick to her lips. Not willing to risk a conversation, Aurelie backed out, turned and spotted the exit sign glowing red over the door at the end of the hallway.

Air.

She needed fresh air to clear her mind and forget what Robin Hood had stolen from her.

A kiss.

He'd stolen a kiss.

Was it theft if she'd kissed him back?

She shot a glance over her shoulder, praying he wasn't following her. In the back of her mind, a devilish thought outweighed the prayer with the hope that he would come after her. If they were out on the boardwalk, away from the guests and backers, she wouldn't embarrass her father, and she wouldn't have to push Robin Hood away so quickly.

Fearing he might follow her out the door, she ran toward the exit and burst through it, out into the open.

She'd wanted fresh air.

But in the deep south of Louisiana, fresh air included almost one hundred percent humidity without cleansing, refreshing rain.

She was immediately struck by the overwhelming humidity that made her sweat immediately.

Well, damn. She didn't want to return to the ballroom and her father's wrath and the curious and intrusive gawking of people who had no right to be all up in her business.

Aurelie spied the boardwalk leading out into the bayou, a recent addition to the Gautreaux Chateau venue that had intrigued her enough to choose this site for her father's fundraiser.

She'd spent so much time arranging for all the deliveries, staffing and guest lists, she hadn't had time to visit the boardwalk and see the amazing vistas in the bayou during the day.

Rather than walk back into the mansion and face all those people—one in particular—Aurelie chose to take the opportunity to walk along the boardwalk, stretching out into the bayou. She struck out at a swift pace, determined to forget Robin Hood and that kiss.

She might have reconsidered if the moon and starlight hadn't chosen that moment to emerge from behind a bank of clouds and shine brightly down on the wooden planks, tempting her with a silvery path through the bayou. Moonlight glinted off the inky black water.

The sound of nature blared louder than the orchestra playing in the ballroom. Anyone who said it was quiet in the countryside didn't live near the bayou. Frogs and crickets sang, their music almost deafening in the night.

Starlight reflected off the bayou. Something moved in the water, like a floating log with twin spots of starlight reflecting off eyes. Alligator.

Aurelie shivered, glad for the boardwalk and the railing to keep her from falling in with the lethal predator.

She'd gone more than fifty yards on the boardwalk, losing sight of the mansion as the path twisted and turned through stands of partially submerged cypress trees with long, lacy branches.

Before she realized she was very alone and out of sight of the chateau, clouds drifted in, blocking the stars and moonlight. Aurelie's steps faltered. The defining sounds of frogs and crickets faded around her, replaced by the sound of footsteps on the boardwalk behind her. Her heart leaped into her throat. Was it him?

She spun to face the man who'd been occupying too much of her thoughts. She lifted her chin, threw back her shoulders and fisted her hands on her hips. With a sarcastic comment poised on her lips, she waited for him to round the corner of the boardwalk and the overhanging limbs of a cypress tree.

At that moment, the clouds moved on, and the moon and stars illuminated the night.

The man rounded the corner, running full-on. Instead of Robin Hood, with his green hat, jacket, tights and that stupid quiver of arrows, a man dressed entirely in black, with a black ski mask covering his head and face, charged toward her.

Shocked, she stood for a fraction of a second, gaping. Then, she spun and ran. She wasn't fast enough and didn't have enough of a head start to escape her pursuer.

He didn't slow until he reached her. Hands grabbed the back of her jacket, yanking her to a stop. She tried to shake free of her jacket, but those hands gripped her body, lifted her into the air and flung her over the boardwalk railing into the bayou.

Like so many who'd encountered a life-threatening experience, the event played out in Aurelie's mind in slow motion. She was flying through the air, over the rail, arms and legs flailing. She hit the water sideways, plunging deep beneath the surface. She hadn't even had time to catch her breath. She floundered, kicking her feet while looking for purchase on the silty bottom, and found none.

Aurelie sank deeper, flapping her arms. A fairly good swimmer, she wasn't so afraid of drowning. Well, as long as she could figure out up from down, and that was proving to be a problem. The bayou here wasn't terribly deep. Her lungs burning, she couldn't find her footing, but she'd seen the eyes of alligators rising above the surface of the water in their nightly search for prey. She had to get out of the water fast. Or she'd become that prey.

WHEN BEAU TURNED AWAY from the ladies' restroom door, he looked right and left. There were no other doors along the corridor except the men's room. He ran in there and checked just in case she'd been dragged inside. He was out in seconds, eyeballing the exit door at the end of the hallway.

She had to have gone outside.

He ran to the exit door and burst out into the night.

He stood for a second, looking right then left. A stone walkway led around the side of the building. He ran down the path that emerged on a wooden platform, which was the beginning of a boardwalk leading out into the bayou.

He stared out at the empty boardwalk.

Surely, she hadn't gone out on the boardwalk alone at night. He glanced all around and didn't see her anywhere in sight.

Fuck.

Beau stepped out onto the boardwalk and ran, praying the boardwalk was the same way out as it was back. If she'd gone out on the boardwalk, he'd either catch up with her or meet her on the way back.

If it made a loop and came back to another location, he'd have to hurry to catch up. *If she was even on the boardwalk.* Either way, he had to make sure.

Despite the pain in his leg, he sprinted, picking up the pace. If she hadn't taken the boardwalk, she could have continued around the side of the house to the front, where anyone could grab her, shove her into a car, and take off. He'd never know it until it was too late.

Beau ran faster, pushing the pain out of his mind. As he rounded a drooping tree branch over the boardwalk, he spotted a large dark figure ahead of him. He heard a woman's scream as that dark figure lifted her into the air and tossed her over the rail of the boardwalk.

Fuck! Fuck! Fuck!

"Hey!" Beau yelled and raced for the attacker.

The man spun toward him for a second, then turned and ran in the opposite direction.

Beau didn't slow until he arrived at the point at which the dark-clad man had thrown a woman into the bayou. Clouds floated over the moon and sky, darkening the world around him. His heart thundered in his chest; his breathing became ragged as he strained to see into the dark abyss. He couldn't see a damned thing, nor could he hear any splashing. Panic threatened to overwhelm him, but he couldn't let it control him. Beau dropped the quiver of arrows, scraped the hat off his head and braced his hands on the boardwalk rail. Before he could think through his actions, he vaulted over the rail into the water. Having grown up in the Bayou, he knew the danger of being in the water at night. Water moccasins were bad enough, but the real threats were the alligators. Splashing noises would have attracted their attention. If there were one or more in the area, which he suspected there were, they'd be angling toward that noise in search of their next meal.

As he sank beneath the surface, he didn't think; he just used his hands to feel for her. She had to be here. He had to bring her up before she drowned, or the alligators got to her. He could not fail. This wasn't a helicopter crash that he had no control over. His actions could influence the outcome. If only he could find her!

Beau came up for air, filled his lungs and gauged his location compared to the boardwalk and the trajectory of the dark man's launch and quickly dove beneath the surface again. Where was she? She had to be here somewhere.

Something kicked at his hand. He yanked it back for a second, thinking maybe it was an alligator's nose, but when it kicked again, he realized it was a foot. He grabbed hold of a boot. Another booted foot kicked him in the head. He grabbed that one, too, and pulled the woman's body toward him in a sharp downward motion.

She fought, kicking and swinging, the water

slowing her movements. Still, it was a struggle to get a good hold of her. His lungs burned with the need for air. Wrapping his arm around her body, he clamped her arms to her side and kicked hard, sending them toward the surface.

As their heads emerged, the woman in his arms dragged air into her lungs, still kicking to keep her head above water. Once she'd taken a breath, she fought to free herself from his hold.

Beau released her.

Her head immediately sank below the surface. She reached for him, dug her fingers into his jacket and clawed her way up his body, pushing him downward as she fought to come up.

Knowing they could both drown if he didn't take control, he knocked her hands aside, spun her around and hooked an arm over her chest, gripping her beneath her opposite arm.

When he could catch his breath, he hissed, "It's me, Robin Hood. Calm down, or we'll both drown." *Or worse*, he wanted to say.

They had to get out of the water.

Her stiff body relaxed against him.

"Are you hurt?" he asked.

"No," she said. "I can swim, but my boots are so heavy."

"It's okay," he reassured her. "I'll keep your head above water. You can help by kicking." Beau looked up at the boardwalk. There had to be steps or a ladder somewhere along its length. They had to have installed some way to get out of the bayou if someone should fall in. Or, as in this case, they were thrown in.

Starlight glinted off metal several yards away from where they tread water. He settled into a side-stroke, dragging Aurelie along with him.

She kicked, helping them move a little faster, but otherwise, let him keep her from going under again.

When he reached the ladder, he stopped. "Can you climb?"

She nodded.

He held onto her until she had a firm grip on the ladder.

Aurelie pulled herself out of the water, one metal bar at a time, until she could get her feet on the bottom rung. When she did, she paused, glanced over her shoulder and yelped. "'Gator!"

Beau looked back to see what looked like a floating log with eyes heading his way—and it was big. Big enough to take on a full-grown man, roll him beneath the surface and hold him there until he drowned.

Heart pounding, Beau held onto the side of the ladder, braced his hand on Aurelie's ass and shoved her upward. "Go! Go! Go!"

As she scrambled up the ladder, he inched out of the water behind her. His legs and feet were still in the water, and the alligator was less than a yard away.

He couldn't wait another second. He climbed up the ladder behind the woman, his arms around her, his legs and feet now clear of the surface. He moved in sync with Aurelie, ascending rung after rung. He was out of the water, out of the alligator's range, and there to catch his client if she missed her footing or slipped and fell.

When they reached the top, he palmed her bottom and gave her enough of a boost to send her over the rail.

She rolled over the top and collapsed onto the boardwalk.

Beau slung his leg over the rail and dropped down beside her, crouched and ready should the man who'd thrown her return to finish the job.

Once he was sure they were alone, he straightened. "All clear," he said, out of habit.

Aurelie drew in a deep breath and let it out slowly. "Good."

Beau held out his hand.

"Thank you for saving my life," she said, laying her palm on his.

"My pleasure," he responded, all civil and calm, although his heart thundered against his ribs, and the panic he'd held at bay returned with a vengeance. He pulled her up with a little more force than necessary.

Aurelie stumbled and fell against him.

Beau encircled her back with his arm and held

her until she was steady on her feet, and he could get his breathing under control.

She stood with her hands resting on his chest, bayou water dripping from her hair. Somewhere along the way, she'd lost the goggles. Moonlight reflected in her dark eyes.

"You really are..." she started and stopped talking, her tongue sweeping across her lips.

Beau's lips twitched on the corners. "Handsome? Tenacious? Striking? Dauntless?" he offered to complete her unfinished sentence.

"I was going to say Peter Pan since Robin Hood never had to battle alligators." Her brow furrowed. "But if you want to go down the path of adjectives, I'd go for egotistical, arrogant and big-headed, especially since you're wearing green tights and you're all wet."

He chuckled and let go of her, letting his arms fall to his sides. "Way to deflate my confidence."

"I'm sure I only made a dent." She stepped back. "But really, thank you." Her gaze went to the bayou.

The gentle swirl of disturbed water highlighted the swish of the alligator's tail as he swam away from his missed meal.

Aurelie shivered and wrapped her arms around herself. "That was close."

"Too close," Beau agreed, thinking not of the alligator but of how much he'd wanted to kiss her and nearly had. He scooped up the quiver of arrows and slung the strap over his shoulders. "Any idea who tossed you into the drink?"

She shook her head. "None. He was dressed all in black, including a black ski mask that covered his face and head. All I know is that he was big."

Beau nodded. "I saw him. I wasn't close enough to stop him from tossing you over the rail."

"I thought I heard someone yell." She stared down at the water again. "Normally, I'm a good swimmer. Not great, but good enough to get myself out of the water." She turned her gaze to him, her brow wrinkling. "I couldn't tell up from down until you brought me to the surface." She gave him a weak smile. "I'm sorry if I fought you. For a moment, I thought you might be the guy who threw me in."

"We made it out," he said. "That's all that matters."

"I guess I'm lucky you were out on the boardwalk when you were." The lines on her forehead deepened. "Why were you out here?"

"I followed you," he said.

"Why?" she asked.

He thought fast. "That kiss," he blurted.

She nodded. "Regrets?"

He shook his head, a smile teasing his lips. "No. Not at all. I wanted to apologize if I embarrassed you in public." Which was true. He didn't regret the kiss. It was the highlight of his otherwise almost disastrous evening.

She stared at him for a long moment. "You didn't

embarrass me," she said. "However, you might have embarrassed my father."

He looked away, his mouth twisting.

"He didn't…" Aurelie touched his arm. "Did my father say something to you about it?"

Beau shrugged. "Nothing I wouldn't expect from a father looking out for his daughter."

"I'll bet it was a little more than a comment. Knowing my father, he probably threatened you with a lawsuit for sexual harassment or something equally ridiculous."

Beau's eyes widened. "Really? I guess I must've gotten off light. I only got the verbal dressing down. No lawsuits or threats of a hitman." He grinned.

Aurelie buried her face in her hands. "Geez. Now, it's my turn to apologize." She lowered her hands. "My father can be a bit overprotective. I'm surprised he hasn't hired a bodyguard to follow me around."

A stab of guilt hit Beau square in the gut. Now would be the time to own up to his real role in the night's event. But he'd promised her father to keep that secret for now.

"Your father must love you a lot to look out for you like he is," he said softly.

She turned away, her arms wrapping around herself again. "He's been that way since my mother died. Even more so since he announced his reelection campaign."

"I'm sorry about your mother," he said. "What happened, if you don't mind my asking?"

Aurelie looked over her shoulder. "She died in an automobile accident." She turned away again. "I was in the same vehicle. She died, and I lived. You don't know how many times I wished it had been me, not her. I told my father how I felt one time. He went ballistic. I've never told anyone how I felt since. People who haven't lived through something like that don't understand."

Beau's heart squeezed so hard in his chest that he could barely breathe. His eyes burned as he reached out, wrapped his arms around her middle and pulled her back against his front. He didn't say a word. Didn't try to turn her to face him, afraid she'd see her emotions reflected in his eyes. Afraid she'd see his tears.

If he could, he'd take away her pain. If he could, he'd take the place of her mother. Die in her place to free Aurelie of the guilt she felt for living when her mother had died.

If he could, he'd take the place of all his team-mates, his friends, his battle buddies who'd died in that helicopter crash.

Holding Aurelie in his arms, he began to realize he'd lived for a purpose. And that purpose was to keep this woman safe.

God, he was even more afraid than ever. Afraid he wouldn't be enough to protect Aurelie Anderson.

CHAPTER 3

Aurelie leaned into Robin Hood, letting him shoulder her burden, if even for a moment. After her father had lost his shit when she'd told him she'd wished she'd died instead of her mother, she hadn't told anyone the same, not even the therapist her father had hired to help her through the trauma of the accident and the grief of losing her mother.

Yet, here she was, spilling her guts to a man whose name she didn't know. A stranger who'd been there when she'd needed a hero to fish her out of the bayou. The man who'd sent her up the ladder before himself with an alligator within striking distance.

She let him hold her. And it wasn't in a sexual, I-want-in-your-pants kind of way that was so often how men treated her. He held her like a friend comforting another friend with no expectation of her returning the favor. No obligation.

He held her like he understood her pain. Her guilt. The man didn't try to make her feel better with platitudes or tell her she shouldn't have those thoughts. He didn't judge. He only held her.

And she let him.

A minute passed. Maybe two. Or five.

Aurelie lost track of time. All she knew was that she didn't want it to end.

The frogs and crickets were once again singing at full throttle. Moonlight shimmered on the water.

"Magical," she murmured.

"The moonlight on the water?" he whispered, his lips so close to her ear she could feel the warmth of his breath.

She nodded. "Magical from up here."

"Otherwise, deadly," he added.

"Yeah." As much as she wanted the moment to go on, they were both wet. Her feet were probably shriveling in her water-logged boots. If she was feeling uncomfortable, she could imagine how he must be feeling in those tights.

"I should get back to the ballroom. My father will be worried."

His arms tightened around her. "And he'll be even more worried when he discovers you've been in the bayou." He released her and took a step backward.

She turned to face him. "At this point, it might be good if I knew your name, other than Peter Pan."

His eyes narrowed. "Robin Hood," he corrected.

"And I would like to know Amelia Earhart's real name."

She held out her hand. "Aurelie Anderson. But I'm guessing you already knew that since your discussion with my father, Senator Anderson."

He dipped his head. "I did. Since you are the senator's daughter, do you want me to call you Miss Anderson?"

She glanced down at her soaked clothing. "I think we're beyond formalities. You can call me Aurelie or Auri."

"Aurelie, it is." He took her hand. "When I'm not Robin Hood, I'm Beau Boyette."

"Beau Boyette," she said, trying his name out on her tongue and liking it. "A very Cajun moniker."

He nodded. "I come from a long line of Cajuns, born and raised in the bayou." He continued to hold her hand. Not so tightly she couldn't easily pull away.

She liked the way his big fingers curled around hers. A little too much. Aurelie let go and clasped her hands together, the warmth from his hand lingering. "Since you were born and raised in the bayou, swimming with the alligators is nothing new."

"I prefer swimming in the daylight. It's easier to spot them." He glanced in the direction of the chateau. "Should we go break the news to your father that someone attacked you and threw you in the bayou?"

She was shaking her head before he finished the

sentence. "Absolutely not. It's a fundraiser. I don't want people leaving early because someone attacked me."

He tilted his head. "What if the attacker goes after other guests?"

Aurelie frowned and started walking back to the chateau. "You have a point. Although, so far, the attacks lately have only been targeting me. I'll notify the security detail and ask them to keep an eye on people coming and going. They can place someone at the entrance to the boardwalk to keep anyone from wandering out in the dark."

"Law enforcement should be made aware of the attempt on your life," he said, falling in step beside her.

"I'll contact the local sheriff and let him know what happened."

"Before or after the event?" Beau asked. "The attacker could be one of the guests."

Another good point. She tapped a finger to her chin, thinking. "I can hand over the guest list to the sheriff and let him check into the backgrounds of those who purchased tickets."

"You really don't want to let your father know?"

"No."

"Then we'll have to leave without checking in with him first," Beau said.

"I'll have the event coordinator pass the word

onto my father that I had a migraine and went home to bed."

"You get migraines often?" Beau asked.

The chateau came into view, lights shining from the windows, the hum of music warring with nature's symphony.

As she arrived on the platform where she'd started her walk that evening, she turned away from the door she'd used to exit the building and walked toward the front. She came to a stop at the second platform that marked the other end of the boardwalk. "My attacker had to have exited the boardwalk here." She studied the side of the chateau, spotting what appeared to be a camera mounted near the eaves. "I wonder if the video camera caught him. If he was still wearing the ski mask, it wouldn't do much good."

"Unless he removed it so as not to draw attention from security or the guests," Beau said.

"I'll ask the event coordinator to let me see the footage tomorrow morning."

"Have security guard that footage. You don't know how sophisticated your attacker might be. He might be one step ahead of you and erase it."

"True." She looked at him through narrowed eyes. "What did you say you do for a living?"

"I didn't," he said and hooked her arm. "Come on. We can get the valet to bring your car around."

She stopped, forcing him to stop as well. "Damn."

"What?"

"I rode with my father." She shook her head. "Not that I would get into his Porche as wet as I am. It might ruin the leather." Her lips twisted. "I could call Uber." She pulled her cell phone out of her pocket and glanced down at the black screen. She tried to reboot it. Nothing.

"Dead, right?" he asked, pulling his phone from his pocket. "Mine, too."

"God, I'm sorry. I'll replace it."

"No. It's an older model. I intended to replace it soon." He slipped the phone back into his pocket and checked his other pocket, pulling out a set of keys. "Thank goodness I didn't lose them in the bayou." Beau looked up. "I could give you a ride to your place in my truck. I don't mind if you get my leather wet. It's a work truck. It's seen worse."

Aurelie frowned. "Get into a truck with a virtual stranger?"

He raised his hands, palms upward. "I'd think saving your life would put us past the stranger category. If it helps, I could call my mother and let her vouch for me."

"You can't," she said, her lips quirking. "Your phone is dead."

Beau sighed. "We could borrow the coordinator's phone. Although, my mother won't answer a strange number, thinking it could be spam."

"Or I could borrow his phone and call for a lift service to pick me up," she suggested.

"You could. And how long would it take for someone to get here? Twenty or thirty minutes? I could get you home in that amount of time."

"How do you know?" She lifted her chin in challenge. "You don't know where I live."

"You're right, but it would be twenty or thirty minutes sooner than anyone having to drive out here in the middle of nowhere to pick you up first." He shrugged. "Your call, but I'll follow you anyway."

Aurelie frowned. "Are you a stalker?"

"No," he said. "But I saved your life. They say when you save a person's life, you're responsible for that person."

She shook her head. "In perpetuity?"

He nodded, his face poker straight. "I take my responsibilities seriously. If someone attacked you here, he could be waiting at your place to finish what he started."

"I've been getting threats in my text messages." She snorted. "I guess I won't be getting more of them anytime soon since my phone is toast."

"What kind of threats?" he asked.

"Actually, death threats." She held up her dead cell phone. "I'd show them to you, but—"

"—you can't." He nodded at the defunct device. "You should get a new cell phone tomorrow, and you might consider changing the number."

"I'd thought about that but haven't had time. I was working on preparations for this event." She sighed. "Okay. I guess since you did save my life, I can trust you to get me to my house." She grimaced. "It's just that you've already done so much for me by pulling me out of the bayou."

"If I didn't want to help, I wouldn't have offered," he said. "Alone, you're too easy a target. Since you're getting death threats, and now someone has acted on those threats, it might help to have someone around. Maybe even deter the attacker."

"I thought the threats would go away," she murmured. "My father wanted to hire a bodyguard for me. Maybe he's right—at least until law enforcement figures out who's behind the threats and the attack."

"It's not a bad idea," he said.

She met his gaze. "What was it you said you do for a living?"

His lips turned upward on the corners. "I didn't. The truth is, I recently separated from the military."

"Really?" She looked at him with new interest. She knew so very little about this man, and she wanted to know so much more. "What branch?"

"Army," he answered.

"You're too young to retire," she said. "Why did you leave?"

He looked away. "Medically retired."

"I'm sorry. And here I've been all about me. That

must've been hard to be processed out." Her brow dipped. "Were you injured on a mission?"

He nodded.

She waited a moment for him to expand on his injury. When he didn't, she let it go. Clearly, he didn't want to talk about it. "Well, I hope rescuing me didn't aggravate your injuries."

"It didn't," he said. "Are you ready to get out of here?"

She nodded. "After we get with security and the event coordinator." After one last glance at her attire, she shook her head. "Let's get it over with."

Together, they walked around to the front of the building, where two security guards stood talking to the event coordinator.

The three men were shocked to learn she'd been attacked on the boardwalk.

Aurelie didn't want to tell them, but they needed to know to keep the guests safe.

"I'll cordon off the access to the boardwalk to keep anyone else from wandering out there," the event coordinator said.

"*After* you inform my father of my departure," she said with a pointed stare. "Tell him I had a migraine and went home to sleep it off."

The man nodded.

"Oh," she added, "and that I caught a ride with one of the guests. Since he will ask, tell him it was with Beau Boyette."

The event coordinator entered the chateau to tell her father of her departure. One of the security guards got on his radio and informed the other guards of what had happened on the boardwalk and told them to keep an eye on all exits and people coming and going. He had one of the guards position himself in the room with the security cameras until the sheriff's department could get there to review the footage.

When Aurelie had done all she could do without actually going back into the chateau, she turned to Beau. "I'd like to stop at the sheriff's office in the nearby town to report the assault before you take me home."

"We can do that." He held out his arm like a gentleman offering to escort a lady dressed in the type of ball gown her father had wanted her to wear.

Aurelie was wet, uncomfortable and too tired to argue. She hooked her hand in the crook of his elbow and allowed him to lead her to a big black pickup on the far end of the parking lot. She figured that if he was going to kill her, he wouldn't have rescued her from drowning or being eaten alive by the alligators in the bayou.

He opened the passenger door, helped her up into the seat and then closed the door.

As she buckled the seatbelt, her gaze followed him around the front of the truck.

His face was ruggedly handsome. Broad shoulders

strained the seams of the Robin Hood costume. And the tights...they emphasized his thickly toned thighs and calves. Men like him should wear tights more often.

Her pulse quickened as he tossed the quiver of arrows into the back seat and climbed into the driver's seat, his thigh that much closer to her. His legs looked amazing in the tights. She wondered how amazing they would look out of them.

Heat coiled low in her belly at the thought of him removing not only the stretchy garment but the jacket and anything else he might have underneath them.

Aurelie tore her gaze away from him and stared at her side window, only to realize it reflected the people in the cab of the truck. She could look at him in the reflection without being so obvious.

He turned to her and winked at her reflection.

Heat filled her cheeks. She faced the front windshield, trying to appear as if she hadn't seen the wink and he hadn't caught her looking at his reflection.

Beau chuckled as he started the engine and shifted into reverse, backing out of the parking space. He drove out of the lot onto the highway, heading toward the nearest town.

For the first couple of minutes, neither of them spoke, giving Aurelie too much time to think of how lucky she was that he'd come to the event that night and that he'd been there to rescue her—which had

her wondering why he'd come to the ball that night
to begin with.

She turned to him, her eyes narrowing. "Tonight's
ball was a fundraiser for my father's reelection."

He nodded. "That's what I understand."

"The guests paid a lot of money for their tickets,
with the money going toward the campaign."

He glanced her way. "Are you going somewhere
with this?"

"You don't strike me as someone who'd pay a lot
of money to go to a masquerade party."

"And yet, I was there, in costume."

"How did you end up with a ticket?"

He gave her a brief smile. "It was given to me."

"Who gave it to you, and why?" she asked, suspicion blossoming.

His gaze went to the road ahead. "Your father
gave me the ticket."

"My father?" Aurelie frowned. "Why? Having just
left the military, I'd think you wouldn't have large
sums of money to contribute to my father's
campaign."

"As a matter of fact, since I was deployed often
and had nowhere to spend my paychecks, I've saved a
considerable amount." His lips pressed into a tight
line. "As to why your father invited me, maybe I was
the obligatory veteran invited to show his support of
the men and women who have served. You'll have to
ask him why he invited me."

She studied him, looking for any body language that would tell her that she shouldn't believe him. Either he had a really good poker face, or he was telling the truth. Still, it didn't make sense that her father had invited the man without telling Aurelie.

She'd ask him the next time she saw him. For the moment, she had no reason to think Beau was lying. Why would he?

The man drove to the sheriff's office and parked out front. She didn't wait for him to open her door but got out on her own and met him at the front of the truck. They entered the office together.

Aurelie gave a deputy a brief description of the attack, the approximate time and what she could convey about the man's appearance.

Beau reported what he'd witnessed.

The deputy recorded the information and their contact information and promised to look into the situation and any video footage that might be obtained from the chateau.

Satisfied that they'd done their due diligence by reporting the crime, they left the sheriff's office.

Again, Beau opened the passenger door for Aurelie and handed her up into the vehicle.

When he slipped into the driver's seat, he started the engine and turned to her. "Where to from here? New Orleans?"

She shook her head. "My father lives in Baton Rouge. He'd prefer if I lived with him, but I moved out when I went to college and only stay with him when I'm working on a special project for him. Mostly, I live in a little house in a small town, close enough to commute to Baton Rouge or New Orleans when the need arises." She grimaced. "The good news is that you don't have to take me to the cities. I live in Bayou Miste," she said.

Beau's eyes widened. "Bayou Miste? Seriously?"

Her frowned. "You say that like it's a bad thing?"

"Not at all. It's just that I have relatives in Bayou Miste."

Her frown deepened. "The same last name? Boyette?"

He nodded.

Her eyes widened. "As in Ben and Alex Boyette?"

He grinned. "Cousins. All nineteen of them."

"Your uncle, the overachiever?" She laughed. "I should've put the names together, but Boyette is a common name."

"My extended family made it a common name by adding to the numbers." He shifted into gear and pulled out of the parking lot.

"Do you know how to get there?"

He nodded. "I could get there with my eyes closed."

"Please," she said. "I'd prefer if you kept them open." She leaned back in her seat, feeling better about getting into a strange man's truck. He was a Boyette, related to the Bayou Miste Boyettes. "I like your cousins," she said. "At least those two. I met them at the Raccoon Saloon with their spouses. I run into them in town or at festivals." She shook her head. "I knew there were a lot of them, but nineteen? Wow."

"The Boyettes believe in big families. My parents drew the line at ten. My mother made my father get snipped after her tenth baby. She only had one set of twins, which meant nine pregnancies."

"You'd think her body would give out by then." Aurelie shook her head again. "I can't imagine how she held up, not to mention your poor aunt."

Beau grinned. "My aunt is in as good or better shape than most of her children. She has to be to keep up with all of them. And she's bound and determined to get them all married off. Ben and Alex were the first two. I think she's working on finding matches for the twins, Dolley and Madison, now."

Aurelie's widened. "Dolley and Madison?"

"My aunt named her children after important historical figures like past presidents, inventors and founding fathers." He glanced toward her. "Ben and Alex are Benjamin Franklin Boyette and Alexandra Belle Boyette."

Aurelie laughed. "I didn't know that. How clever. What about your family? Did your parents do that as well? I mean, Beau isn't a name I recognize as a historical figure."

He shook his head. "No, my mother is a Cajun

through and through. She gave all her children good old Cajun-French names." He turned off the main highway onto the road that would take them to the small town of Bayou Miste as if he'd done it a hundred times. "I haven't been back here since I was on leave for Ben's wedding. That's been a few years."

"I've met his wife. She's a beauty and really nice. She gave me a charm to ward off evil."

Beau's eyebrows rose. "She did? Are you sure that's what it's for?"

"That's what she said. Why?"

"You know she's the granddaughter of Bayou Miste's Voodoo Queen, don't you?"

"I might have heard that," she said, trying to remember who might have told her. "So?" She stared at him. "You don't believe in Voodoo, do you?"

He shrugged. "I'm not going to say I don't. All I'm saying is there've been some things that have happened in the bayou that can't be explained away with science."

"Well, I don't believe in magic."

"Do you still have the gris-gris Lucie gave you?"

"Yes. It was a gift. I couldn't just throw it away."

He slowed as he passed the battered shack, with a sign hanging over the door proclaiming it the Raccoon Saloon.

"Some things never change," he murmured. "I'm surprised that building hasn't fallen down."

Aurelie chuckled. "Me, too. But that doesn't scare

people away. The parking lot is always full on the weekends."

When he drove into Bayou Miste, he pointed at his aunt's house.

Aurelie told him where to turn, and soon, he pulled into the gravel driveway of the little cottage she'd painted robin's egg blue with a pastel yellow door.

She sighed as he shifted into park. This was her home, the very first and only house she'd ever signed a mortgage on. "Thank you for bringing me home." Aurelie pushed open her door.

He opened his door as well.

"You don't have to walk me to the door," she said.

He ignored her statement and met her at the front of his truck with his hand held out. "The key?"

"I left my purse in my father's car." Despite her admission, she climbed the stairs. "But I keep a spare under the flowerpot next to the—" she stopped short of the door, her brow furrowing.

The flowerpot she'd planted full of petunias lay in pieces, dirt scattered across the porch, flowers uprooted and dying. The key was gone, and the front door stood slightly ajar.

Beau stepped in front of her. "Get in the truck."

When she didn't move immediately, he spoke louder, "Get in the truck. Now!"

Aurelie jerked to attention and started down the porch stairs.

Beau moved with her, backing down the porch steps without turning his back on the semi-opened door.

Aurelie hurried toward the truck, climbed into the passenger seat and waited for Beau to get into the other side.

He didn't get into the driver's seat. Instead, he reached beneath the seat and pulled out a very lethal-looking handgun.

Beau met her gaze across the console. "I want you to get into the driver's seat as soon as I close the door. If I'm not back in three minutes, drive to the sheriff's office in town for help."

"You're scaring me," Aurelie said, her voice shaking. "If you think someone might be inside my house, come with me to the sheriff's office. Let them handle it."

"Driver's seat." He closed the door and waited for a second before saying loud enough she could hear through the glass. "Now."

Aurelie scrambled across the console, banged her knee on the steering wheel and let out a string of curses as she watched Beau circle around to the back of the house.

Her pulse hammered through her veins as she counted the seconds for the first minute. Then, the second minute. She'd made it halfway through the third minute when Beau emerged from the front door and waved for her to join him.

She flung open the door and dropped to the ground. Her knees shook so much she nearly collapsed. Then, she was running toward Beau. When she reached him, she hurled herself into his arms. "That was the longest two and a half minutes of my life. What took you so long?"

He held her for a moment, his cheek pressed to her temple. "You can't stay here tonight."

She leaned back and stared up into his face. "Why?"

He stepped back and pushed the door wide with the barrel of his handgun.

She stepped across the threshold, and her heart plunged to the pit of her belly.

Every piece of furniture she'd so lovingly selected for her little house was either shredded or broken, undeniably destroyed beyond any chance of fixing.

But worse...the red spray-painted letters on the walls made Aurelie shake with a combination of residual fear after being thrown in the bayou and white-hot, blinding rage.

DIE BITCH.

CHAPTER 4

"COME ON. You can't stay here." Beau gripped Aurelie's arm and urged her toward the door.

"This is my house." She shook free of his hand and stared at the destruction, her eyes glistening with unshed tears. "How could someone do this?"

"I don't know. There's plenty of trouble in this world without making more here at home." He touched her arm. "We need to report this to the sheriff."

"Damn right, we do." She reached for a photo frame lying on the floor, the glass broken, but the picture still intact.

He stopped her before she could pick it up. "Don't touch anything," he said. "They'll want to dust for fingerprints. Maybe they can find a match in the criminal databases."

She stared at the photograph. "We took that

picture of the three of us on our last vacation together before my mother died." Her fists clenched at her sides as she drew in several ragged breaths. "Bastard!"

"Since neither of us have functioning cell phones, we have to go to the sheriff's office." When she didn't move, Beau added, "I'm not leaving you here. You have to come with me."

"Okay." She drew in another breath and let it out slowly. "I don't suppose I can grab some toiletries and clothes?" She shook her head even as she said the words. "Yeah. Probably not. Leave it as is and let the sheriff sort through the evidence."

She spun on her booted heels and marched out the door without looking back.

Beau followed, using his foot to pull the door closed behind him, not wanting to touch the door-knob in case a print could be lifted off its surface.

Aurelie climbed up into the passenger seat of his pickup, her face set in stone, a muscle ticking in her jaw. "Bastard!" she muttered again. "I hope he burns in hell."

Beau slid into the driver's seat, backed out of the driveway and onto the street. After one last glance, he drove to the sheriff's office in Bayou Miste. They spent the next hour with a deputy reporting the inci-dent, giving their fingerprints and filling him in on everything that had led up to the break-in.

By the time they were done, Aurelie's shoulders

were drooping, and shadows had formed beneath her eyes.

Once they were back in his truck, Beau shifted into drive and headed out of Bayou Miste.

"I don't even have my purse. It's in my father's car," Aurelie said. "No phone. No credit cards. No house." Tears welled and spilled down her cheeks. With an angry swipe of her hand, she brushed them away, her lips pressing into a thin line. "I guess I could go stay with my father. God, he's going to be horrified and insist I move back in with him permanently." She pushed her hand through her hair. "I love my father, but I want a life of my own."

"It's getting late," Beau said. "You can stay at my place for the night. We can figure things out in the morning."

She turned her head toward him, giving him a skeptical frown. "Your place... We..." She shook her head. "This isn't your problem. It's mine. You've already done enough. Just drop me off at the nearest homeless shelter. I'll be all right."

Beau chuckled. "Right. That's not going to happen."

Leaning her head back against the seat, she closed her eyes. "I should've had Lucie's charm on me tonight, and maybe none of this would've happened."

"I thought you didn't believe in Voodoo."

"If it keeps me out of trouble, I might start believing." Her head popped up. "Seriously, you should've left me at the sheriff's office. They might have an empty cell they could let me sleep in tonight. It's that or drive me to Baton Rouge to stay with my father. Forget it. It's too far." Her head moved from side to side. "I'm so fucking tired I could sleep in your truck. What do you say? I promise not to drool on your leather."

"You're not staying in my truck. It's too far and too late to go to Baton Rouge. I'll say again, you can stay at my place. It's not much, and it'll only be for the night. Tomorrow, we'll find an alternative."

"Where is your place?" she asked. "I know so little about you besides the fact your family is extremely fertile."

"I'm staying in a boarding house not terribly far from here."

"Oh." She frowned without opening her eyes. "A boarding house?"

"I told you I recently left the military. I'm still looking for a more permanent place to live. You can have the bed; I'll sleep on the floor." He sighed. "And no, I'm not a pervert who'll jump you in your sleep. If you prefer, I can sleep outside the door to my room. You can lock yourself in."

She chewed on her bottom lip for a moment before asking, "Where is this boarding house?"

"Bayou Mambaloa," he answered.

"That's not far."

"No, it's not. It's where I grew up."

"You left the service and came home," she said softly.

He nodded. "That's right. If I know my mother, she'll find a place for you to stay while your place is being investigated, cleaned up and restored."

Aurelie snorted. "And to think, I chose Bayou Miste to get away from the crime in the cities."

"While we're looking for a place for you to stay, we need to be thinking about who has it in for you," he said. "Who did you piss off so badly that they want you dead?"

"I'm sure there are a number of people," she said.

"Why?"

"My work for my father's philanthropy puts me crossways with corporations, business owners and the Cajun mafia."

"Damn." Beau shot a glance her way. "What philanthropy is that?"

"My father loves this state and wants to do right by it and the people who live here. He's vowed to do everything in his power to preserve the bayou for future generations."

"And how does that make people hate you?" Beau asked.

"I'm an environmental advocate. I look for corporations violating EPA guidelines. For example, those companies dumping toxins into the bayou..." She waved a hand in the air. "I gather evidence and blow the whistle on them. Sometimes, the businesses are fined and forced to get it right and clean up their mess. Other times, they're shut down, and the people who work there are out of jobs."

"I can see where that would make you unpopular," Beau said. "Why does your father have you do the dirty work?"

"He didn't want me to; I insisted." She gave an abrupt laugh. "Stupid, huh?"

"Not stupid," he said. "Obviously, you care."

"I love my state as much as my father. I hate seeing it destroyed by people who ignore the rules put in place to protect it. I don't set out to close down businesses and cost people their livelihoods. If the corporations would follow the guidelines and quit cutting corners that end up poisoning the bayous, I could go to work in a souvenir shop selling keychains to tourists and be perfectly happy."

"Why isn't the EPA doing the so-called dirty work?" Beau asked.

"They aren't seeing what I'm seeing," she said. "The companies do just enough to cover their tracks while the EPA agents are there, then they go back to their destructive ways once the agents' backs are turned."

"What has happened recently that would make someone come after you with such a vengeance?"

Aurelie shrugged. "That's what's crazy. My work hasn't shut down anyone recently."

Beau frowned. "When did you start getting death threats?"

"I got the first one two weeks ago."

"Did anything in your life happen two weeks ago that might've triggered the hate?"

She shook her head. "I've been busy with my father's campaign since he formally announced his run for reelection. He was teetering on a decision to retire but finally decided he was all in for another term."

"When did he make the formal announcement?"

"Three weeks ago, give or take a day or two." Her brow furrowed. "You think the death threats against me have to do with my father's reelection?"

"The timing seems to indicate it could be."

"But why go after me?" She held up a hand. "Not that I'd want them to target my father. But if someone doesn't want my father to run, you'd think they'd go after him."

"Would that be too obvious?" Beau suggested. "Who's his opponent?"

"Jason Gousman," Aurelie said. "He's a corporate attorney out of New Orleans, running on a bring-more-jobs to Louisiana platform. He's younger than my father, good-looking and charismatic, but youth, looks and charisma aren't everything."

"Sometimes, it is," Beau said. "Especially if the voters are bombarded with his name and face in advertisements."

Aurelie sighed. "And it's our job to educate the voters about what they're getting in my father. Gousman has only worked for major corporations. He claims it makes him perfect for negotiating deals to move production facilities into the state. He doesn't have a track record for public works or representing the people like my father does."

"It can be an uphill battle to educate voters who are more worried about paying the rent than getting out to vote."

"I know." Her lips pressed together. "Though our work to preserve the natural resources has caused some job loss, my father has brokered deals with major corporations to bring their foreign operations to the state. He's worked to get them tax incentives while they're establishing their operations. They brought jobs. Employed Louisianans."

Beau laughed. "You're preaching to the choir." He slowed to a stop and shifted into park in front of the boarding house. Hank Patterson, the founder of the Brotherhood Protectors, had purchased it to provide temporary housing for the new team of men hired to staff the Bayou division. It gave them and new hires a place to live until they could secure more permanent lodging. "We're here."

Aurelie sat up. "You weren't kidding when you said you were staying at a boarding house. It looks like something out of the early nineteen hundreds."

"Probably because it is." He pushed open his door

and dropped to the ground. Aurelie met him in front of the truck and walked with him to the front entrance. "How many people live here?"

"Six, at last count."

"Male-female ratio?" she questioned.

"All men."

She stopped and faced him. "Is this going to be a problem bringing a woman into an all-male boarding house?"

"It's only all-male because there aren't any women renting rooms here at this time." Which was one hundred percent true. He didn't tell her that the men all worked for the Brotherhood Protectors. Hopefully, he wouldn't run into any of them. If he did, they might blow his cover. He would talk with Senator Anderson tomorrow and see if he would reconsider telling his daughter why Beau Boyette was following her around like a shadow. Lying by omission was as bad as bold-faced lying, and the longer it went on, the madder Aurelie would be when she found out.

"It's just for the night." He opened the door and held it for Aurelie. "We'll find suitable accommodations for you tomorrow."

Her frown remained, denting her forehead with her displeasure.

Beau couldn't blame her. A lone female in a house full of six men was enough to make any woman want to turn around and run.

"I'll make sure no one bothers you," he whispered

as they entered the foyer. "Including me." He cupped her elbow gently, led her up the staircase to the second level and turned right. His room was the last one on the left. They made it all the way to his door before the door they'd just passed opened.

His teammate, Rafael Romero, poked his head out. "I thought I heard someone." He grinned, his eyebrows rising. "Well, well. Who do we have here?" He came out of his room wearing a black T-shirt, gym shorts and nothing else. A strand of black hair fell over his forehead, giving him a rakish charm.

Beau tensed as his teammate turned up the wattage of his smile.

Rafael held out a hand. "I'm Rafael Romero. And who is this vision of loveliness?"

Beau wanted to punch the man in the face for his blatant flirting. All women found him hard to resist.

Aurelie laughed. "Seriously? My makeup is probably smeared, my clothes are still damp, my hair is a mess and I smell like swamp water. Save your flowery words for the giddy girls who probably fall for them. Aurelie Anderson." She gripped his hand, shook it and released it quickly. "Now, I'd like to shower before the stench becomes permanent."

Not to be deterred, Romeo chuckled. "A woman with class and sass. I like it."

Beau stepped between Aurelie and Romeo. "I wouldn't mess with her if I were you," he said. "She's had a rough night."

"If she's hanging with you, I can understand completely." His eyes rounded. "Oh, wait... Is she—"

"Senator Anderson's daughter?" Beau jumped in before Romeo could call her his client. "Yes. And we'd appreciate it if you didn't say anything about her being here."

Romeo met Beau's gaze. "Got it." He made a motion like he was zipping his lips together. "I won't say a word." He turned his smile on Aurelie again. "But if you happen to be at the local bar, I'd like to buy you a drink. You can tell me why my pal Beau made your evening so rough." He winked, lifted her hand and brushed a quick kiss across her knuckles. As quickly as he'd appeared, he disappeared into his room.

Aurelie's gaze followed Romeo until that door closed between them. She faced Beau with a twisted brow. "Is your friend always so..."

"Annoying? Repulsive? Cheesy?" he suggested. "Yes."

"I was going to say suave, charming and effusive." She lifted her shoulders. "But cheesy fits."

Beau used a key to unlock his door, pushed it open and stood back, waiting for her to enter.

Aurelie gave him a narrow-eyed glance as she entered his room.

He glanced over her shoulder. Had he left it tidy that morning? He usually did, but he'd gotten the call for the protector job right after his workout, and he couldn't remember if he'd tossed his sweaty clothes into the clothes basket or onto the bathroom floor.

Once she was inside the bedroom, he slipped through the door and closed it behind him. "I just want to grab a few things and be out of here. You can have the room to yourself."

"Are you really going to sleep on the floor outside that door?" Her brow dipped low on her forehead.

"Yes, ma'am. As you've pointed out, we're strangers. I don't want to make you feel uncomfortable by insisting on sleeping in the same room, even if I slept on the floor. You don't know me from Adam." He crossed to the sturdy oak dresser and pulled out a couple of T-shirts, two pairs of shorts and one set of boxer briefs. On second thought, he grabbed a second set of boxer briefs.

After separating the items, he handed a T-shirt, boxer briefs and shorts to Aurelie. "It isn't sexy lingerie, but you can wear them to sleep in and feel comfortable wearing them out of the room tomorrow. You might have to cinch up the waistband to keep the shorts from falling off."

She took the stack of clothes from his hands. "Thank you. I'll get these back to you when I can get to my own clothes."

"No hurry," he assured her, then ducked into the bathroom, calling over his shoulder. "Fresh towels under the sink. Toothpaste in the drawer, new toothbrush still in the package in the same drawer. You can use my brush. It's in the second drawer. Help yourself. Shampoo in the shower. If you need conditioner, sorry. We can pick up some tomorrow."

Aurelie winced. "Yeah. I'll need some to get through all the tangles."

"If you don't need anything else, I'll be just a few steps away."

"Don't you want to shower the bayou water off you?" she asked.

"When you're done. I know you're uncomfortable in your wet clothes and boots. Take a long hot shower. Let me know when you're done, and I'll jump in to rinse off."

He crossed to the entrance. "Don't stand in the windows. The light from the room will silhouette your body, making it a perfect target to aim for. Again, I'll be close. Just yell."

She nodded.

Beau backed into the hallway, his gaze locked with hers as he pulled the door closed.

While she showered, he'd pull in the big guns. If tonight was any indication of what more was to come, he needed to bring his team in to help solve the mystery of who was terrorizing Aurelie. Between law enforcement and the assets available in the Brotherhood Protectors, they should be able to nail the guy sooner rather than later.

Preferably before the bad guy nailed the beautiful and feisty senator's daughter.

CHAPTER 5

KNOWING BEAU WAS JUST as uncomfortable in his wet boots and clothes as she was, Aurelie hurried into the bathroom, carrying the clothes the man had loaned her.

She lifted them to her nose and inhaled. They smelled like Beau. A woodsy scent she wouldn't soon forget.

After turning on the shower and adjusting the temperature, Aurelie kicked off her boots and peeled the damp socks off her feet. Her toes were cold and pruned from being wet for so long. She couldn't complain. Her toes might be wrinkled, but she was alive. She had been struggling to find her footing and could have drowned had Beau not jumped into the alligator-infested bayou to pull her out.

Her heart swelled in her chest. What he'd done was pretty damn heroic. She smiled. If she called him a hero to his face, he would probably disagree and say he'd done what any man would have done.

Aurelie wasn't that sure. Many of the men she knew wouldn't jump into a dark swamp full of alligators to save their mothers, much less a stranger.

She stripped out of the jacket, shirt and trousers she'd worn as Amelia Earhart and shucked her bra and panties. Leaving the costume on the tile floor, she carried the undergarments into the shower with her. The sooner she hand-washed them, the sooner they'd dry so she could wear them the next day.

Her nipples tingled under the shower's pelting spray. She always left the house in appropriate undergarments. Her mother had drilled it into her to make a habit of wearing a good bra and panties in case she was in an accident, and the paramedics had to cut off her clothes.

Aurelie always thought that would be terribly embarrassing. But if it meant the difference between life and death, keeping or losing a limb, she prayed they'd cut off the clothes whether her bra and panties were pretty or not.

If her bra and panties didn't dry by morning, could she go commando?

The idea of going without undergarments was new...and surprisingly titillating.

She gripped the bar of soap, worked up a lather in her hands and ran them over her skin, starting with her face, then working her way down her neck, over her shoulders and across her breasts. As her fingers skimmed her nipples, her breath caught in her throat. An image of Beau's big hands grazing the sensitive tips made her core heat, molten hot.

Sliding her soapy hand lower, she cupped her sex and dipped a finger into her channel.

Oh, yeah. Not only was she hot in the middle of a shower, but she was also dreaming lusty dreams about a man who had no intention of charging in to satisfy her sudden urge.

She could call out to him and offer to let him shower at the same time as she did, thus saving water and accomplishing the task twice as fast.

Aurelie was shocked by herself even considering showering with the stranger. She'd never showered with a man.

While no virgin, she hadn't done much sexual exploration. The men she'd slept with had been in a hurry to get to their orgasms. Not one had been too concerned about satisfying her needs. The only real orgasms she'd had were the ones she'd elicited during her own forays into self-satisfaction. That's right...masturbation. Sometimes, with BOB, her battery-operated boyfriend.

She wondered if Beau was the kind of guy who would go straight for his enjoyment or if he would put in the necessary effort to please her. Would he get impatient? Would she have to fake an orgasm, or would Beau get her there?

What was she thinking? It wasn't like they were going to go there. He'd saved her life and felt responsible for her. That didn't mean he was responsible for her orgasms.

Aurelie set the soap in the soap dish, squirted shampoo into her hand and washed the bayou water out of her hair. She rinsed all the soap from her hair and body, turned off the water and grabbed a towel.

After drying off, she pulled on the boxer briefs, liking the way they hugged her hips. Knowing Beau had worn them made her sex tingle and heat swirl low in her belly.

She had to get over her improper thoughts, or she'd have difficulty looking him square in the eye. He might read her mind and be appalled at the sexual content that included him.

When she pulled the T-shirt over her head and let it fall over her naked breasts, a moan escaped her lips before she could stop it.

"Are you all right in there?" Beau called out.

"I'm fine," she answered, her voice high-pitched, strained by her attempt to sound normal when she was having anything but normal feelings for the man on the other side of the door.

"Get a grip," she muttered softly.

"What did you say?" Beau asked, his voice barely muffled by the wood-paneled door.

"Nothing," she said. "Just talking to myself."

Aurelie stepped into Beau's gym shorts, pulled

them up over the boxer briefs, wrapped her hair in a towel and pulled the door open. "It's all yours."

Beau stood in the middle of the room, his chest and feet bare, holding a pair of shorts, a comb and a brush.

He handed her the comb and brush. "If you have trouble getting the tangles out, I can help after I get my shower." His lips twisted. "My younger sisters swear I have a magic touch with tangles."

Aurelie took the comb and brush, grimacing. Without conditioner, the tangles would be almost unbearable. "I might take you up on that," she said.

"Good." Beau stepped around her, his naked shoulder brushing against her arm. "I won't be long."

That brief, skin-to-skin contact shot a spark of electricity up her arm and throughout her body, leaving Aurelie breathless.

Thankfully, he entered the bathroom and closed the door before she gasped.

"Okay," she whispered, very aware of the fact the bathroom door did little to muffle noise. "He's just a man. A stranger. One you might not see again after tomorrow. Get through the night and move on."

The self-pep talk did little to cool the heat burning through her. There was no way she could let him work the tangles out of her hair. He'd be close enough to touch. She wasn't sure she could control her raging hormones.

Pulling the towel off her head, she dug the brush

into her damp hair, yanking at the tangles, hoping the pain would put the kibosh on the lust blossoming inside before the man emerged from the bathroom.

She could hear when he turned on the water, the sound of the shower curtain rings sliding across the metal bar and a deep, soft humming sound.

Curious, she pressed her ear to the door. Her head jerked back as she recognized the tune.

Beau was humming the Elvis song they'd danced to at the chateau. The dance he'd ended with that kiss.

"Can't help Falling in Love," echoed in Aurelie's head as she spun away and tugged again at the tangles refusing to release. She had to get through them before he came out. If she didn't, and he insisted on working through them, she couldn't be responsible for her reactions.

Her hand yanked at the brush. It caught in a tangle and bounced back against her head. When she tried to pull it free, she couldn't. Her hair had wrapped all around the brush.

"Damn," she cursed and tried to work the strands of hair free, one at a time, only making it worse. "Double damn."

"Hey," Beau called out. "Just stop there."

She spun to face him.

He crossed the room, wearing just the gym shorts, nothing else. Droplets of water glistened on his skin, some trapped in the smattering of curls across his chest.

Aurelie's mouth went dry. Holy hell. The less the man wore, the more handsome he got. She'd bet he'd look like amazing completely naked.

She ran her tongue across her dry lips as he reached her, her gaze rising to his.

He was frowning. "Don't," he said, his voice sounding a little choked.

"Don't what?" she whispered, barely able to push air past her vocal cords with him standing close enough she could smell that woodsy scent. Her gaze dropped to his mouth, and her tongue swept across her lips again.

"Do that," he said.

"Do what?" she said, unable to look away from his mouth, wondering if a second kiss would be equally as amazing as that first on the dance floor. If she moved half of a step closer, she could find out for herself. She licked her lips again.

"Licking your lips." Beau gripped her arms, sending shocks of electricity through all over again.

Her pulse slammed through her veins, pounding so hard against her eardrums she could barely hear herself think. She frowned and looked up into his eyes, not exactly sure what he was talking about.

"You're licking your lips, and it's making me crazy," he said softly.

"Sorry." She bit down on her bottom lip. "Does it bother you?"

He chuckled. "More than you know." With his hands still on her arms, he turned her around. "Let me take care of the brush." He guided her to a desk, pulled out a chair and urged her to sit.

She dropped onto the seat, glad to take the weight off her wobbling legs.

Beau's hands went to her hair and the brush knotted in the long tresses.

"I don't know what happened," she said. "One minute, I was brushing, and the next minute, the brush was wadded up in the tangles. I'm not usually so clumsy."

"It's okay," he said, his tone as soothing as his hands.

Moments later, he had the brush free and began working through the knots slowly and patiently. He took his time, careful not to yank too hard and hurt her.

Aurelie closed her eyes and let him wield his magic. She could tell when he'd loosened the last knot and fully expected him to stop.

He smoothed the brush through her hair, over and over. The soothing repetition lulled Aurelie into a trance. She must have fallen asleep and started dreaming. In that dream, Beau alternated between brushing and kissing her hair.

In her dream, she leaned her head back against his

bare belly. His kiss skimmed her lips. She wanted to reach up and pull him closer. Deepen the kiss. Take it to the next level.

The brushing stopped, and the dream kisses stopped.

"All done," he said, his voice deep and resonant.

Aurelie blinked her eyes open, wanting to tell him to kiss her again. But that had been in her dream, right?

Beau reached around her and laid the brush on the desk. "I'll leave it here in case you need it again." He spun away from her, grabbed a pillow from the bed and held it in front of him as he hurried for the door. "I'll be outside the door if you need me. All you have to do is yell."

Then he dove through the door and pulled it closed behind him.

The room cooled by several degrees without his presence.

Or did her body cool?

Aurelie drew in a deep breath and let it out slowly. Had she fallen asleep? She touched her fingers to her lips.

They still tingled from the dream, much like they had after he'd kissed her at the chateaux.

She stared at the door, tempted to open it and ask him if his kisses had been a dream or if they'd been real.

Aurelie rose from the desk chair and was halfway

across the room before she stopped. If the kisses had been a dream, the question would reveal to him what she'd been dreaming about. He'd think her pathetic. Would he kiss her again out of pity?

If the kisses had been real...

That could ignite something she wasn't sure she was prepared to commit to.

Something...? Like what?

A one-night stand?

The few times Aurelie had engaged in sex, she'd been in a committed relationship. Granted, she'd ended up breaking up with the men when they hadn't satisfied her physical or emotional needs. She'd wondered if she was destined to be disappointed by sex. Maybe she was...what was it one of her boyfriends had called her...?

Frigid.

Aurelie crossed her arms over her breasts as she stood staring at the door. She was hot, inside and out. Her pulse raced, pushing molten blood through her veins.

Most definitely not frigid. Not now, anyway.

She took another step toward the door. If she felt this strongly toward her Robin Hood before they had sex, how would she feel during?

Her feet carried her a couple more steps, propelling her toward the man who'd piqued her sexual curiosity.

As if of its own accord, her hand wrapped around the knob.

The cautious, logical voice in her head warned her to think about it. But she could barely hear that voice, like it was coming to her from the deep, dark depths of a cave. The irrational, impulsive woman she'd suppressed for most of her life as a politician's daughter activated the muscles in her hand and twisted the knob, pulling it open before logic could engage.

Beau had been sitting across the hall with his back to the wall, the pillow lying across his lap. As soon as the door opened, he was on his feet in a split second. "What's wrong?"

Impulsive Aurelie conveniently lost her voice.

Logical Aurelie scrambled with a reason for her to open the door. "You."

He frowned. "Me?"

Aurelie dragged her gaze from his and down to the pillow he held in front of him. "You can't sleep in the hallway. It's not fair." She looked around for inspiration. "You should sleep in your own bed. I can curl up in the chair by the window."

He was shaking his head before she finished her sentence. "No way. I'm fine out here. Remember, I was in the Army. Anything is better than a foxhole."

"I won't sleep, knowing you're lying on the floor outside the door. What if someone sneaks up on you trying to get to me? If you're asleep, you might not hear him." She shook her head again.

"Trust me," he said. "I'll hear him."

"But I won't sleep at all, feeling guilty about taking your bed."

"I'm fine," he said. "It's just one night. Go to bed, Aurelie."

She crossed her arms over her chest, her lips pressing into a hard line. "Either sleep in your own bed, or I'll walk out this door and take care of myself. I'm not your responsibility. You can't make me stay."

He held her gaze for a long moment. Finally, he sighed. "How about a compromise?"

"As long as it involves you sleeping in your own room," she lifted her chin, "I'm listening."

"I'll sleep in my room," he said, "on the floor. That way no one will sneak up on me. They'd have to break down the door to get to me or you. That would give me time to react."

Her eyes narrowed. "You'll sleep in your bed."

"On the floor, or I'll stay out here." His lips twitched. "Take it or leave it."

"For God's sake, take it!" a voice called out from behind Romeo's door. "Some of us want to sleep."

Aurelie's cheeks heated. She gripped Beau's arm and dragged him through the door.

He turned and threw the deadbolt.

"If you're insistent about sleeping on the floor, at least take this..." Aurelie hurried toward the bed, pulled the thick comforter off, folded it in half and laid it on the floor at the foot of the bed. The room was small. The man was big. He'd take up most of the floor space. But it was that or the bed. With her.

Her heart stuttered and then raced as she slipped between the sheets and pulled the top one up to her chin.

Beau's lips twisted. "If you're that scared of me, it would be better if I stayed out in the hall."

"I'm not scared of you," she said. She wasn't. She was afraid of her reaction to him, which had her hiding behind the sheet. She was afraid she'd do something dumb like ask him to make love to her.

Beau held up his hand like he was swearing in at a court case. "I promise, you're safe with me. I won't hurt you. I won't touch you." He dropped to the pallet on the floor, flung the pillow behind his head and stared up at the ceiling. Then he added, "Unless you want me to."

Aurelie stiffened. Now, why did he have to go and add that little phrase to his promise?

She flopped back on her pillow and stared up at the ceiling like Beau.

Unless you want me to.

What did he mean by that? Did he want to touch her? Was that his way of letting her know he was interested?

She started to sit up and ask him what he meant but forced herself to lay still.

No. It wasn't an invitation.

He'd said it in jest. He wasn't serious. And she wasn't curious enough to test his theory.

Or was she?

She rolled onto her side, the side facing Beau, and stared down at him.

Beau stared up at the ceiling, his hands laced behind his neck. "What?" he asked, his gaze shifting to hers.

Put on the spot, she lost her nerve and searched for another reason to be on her side facing him. "Just needed to turn off the light." She reached for the black knob up under the lampshade. It was further away than she could manage lying down. Leaning up on her elbow, she strained to reach the little knob.

Just...about...there...

Her elbow slipped over the edge of the mattress. With all her weight poised over that elbow, she went over the edge with it and crashed down on top of Beau.

He grunted as she landed on his chest, knocking the air from his lungs. His arms came around her.

"Oh," she said. "I'm sorry. I didn't mean to..." Planting her hands on his chest, she pushed up. Her knees dropped to the floor on either side of him, and she sat up, straddling his hips, becoming immediately aware of the hard ridge beneath his shorts.

His hands closed around her arms, steadying her. "Are you okay?"

She nodded, her face burning. "I should be asking you that question. I landed on you while trying to reach the light switch..." Aurelie looked up at the damned switch. Meanwhile, the hard ridge beneath her had all her attention. "Are you all right?" *Because you feel mighty fine to me.*

Holy hell, she'd almost spoken that last thought out loud.

"Actually," he said. "I'm not fine."

She frowned, her glance shooting to his eyes. "No?"

"No," he said, his lips forming a thin line. He shifted beneath her, his cock pressing against her sex. "I should sleep out in the hall." With his hands still on her arms, he tried to lift her off him.

She resisted. "Why? Because of this?" She wiggled her bottom, letting him know she knew he was aroused.

His jaw tightened to the point it twitched. He breathed in and out several times before saying, "Yes."

She raised an eyebrow in challenge. "Then why don't you do something about it?"

"I promised not to touch you," he said.

"Didn't you say *Unless you want me to?*" She lifted her chin. Then she lowered her voice to whisper, "What if I want you to?"

CHAPTER 6

Beau stared up into Aurelie's eyes.

He'd tried to shift her off his engorged cock. Tried to control his baser instincts, but the woman had made him crazy with lust when she'd been lying on the bed above him.

Perched on top of him, her sex pressing against his boner, he couldn't think with the head on his shoulders when all the blood shot south to the head of his dick.

He drew in a deep, steadying breath and let it out before saying, "Let me get this straight..." His cock strained against the clothing between him and her sex. "Are you saying you *want* me to...touch you?" He held his breath, his body wanting her to say *Hell yeah,* while what was left of his functioning brain cells warned him that making love to her was a bad idea.

She didn't know he was her bodyguard. He worked for her father. It wasn't in the Brotherhood Protector's handbook, not that there was one, but he was pretty certain fucking the client was against the rules.

Aurelie shrugged. "It crossed my mind."

Whoa. Beau's mind exploded with flashing red lights and a screeching warning system. *Put on the brakes. Abort mission.*

She hadn't said yes.

He sat up, lifting her off him at the same time and setting her to the side.

"Wait," she said. "What did I say?"

He pushed to his feet. "It's what you didn't say," he murmured. Beau gathered the comforter and the pillow and stepped past Aurelie, where she sat on the floor, frowning up at him.

"But—" She pushed to her knees.

"Goodnight, Miss Anderson." He practically raced for the door, grabbed the knob and twisted. When it didn't open, he remembered he'd engaged the dead-bolt. He flipped the lever, yanked open the door and bolted through. "Lock the door," he threw over his shoulder, refusing to look back at the woman who had his cock so hard he was sure he'd be awake all night with blue balls.

Better that than to make love to the pretty client with hair he'd run his fingers through. He knew he shouldn't have kissed her when she'd fallen asleep while he'd smoothed out her tangles. Since kissing her on the dance floor, he couldn't resist kissing her again.

Kissing was relatively harmless.

Making love to her took harmless to an entirely different level. Her father, the senator, might sic his lawyers on him for breach of contract or whatever he could get to stick. He'd have him up on some felony charges for taking advantage of his daughter.

Her father wasn't the worst of it. He couldn't make love to Aurelie. Most likely, she'd be angry when she found out he wasn't just a guy who'd randomly followed her out onto that boardwalk. She'd be livid when she discovered he hadn't been completely truthful with her.

No woman loved a liar.

He could argue that he hadn't actually lied to her.

She wouldn't buy it. Lying by omission was still lying.

He tossed the comforter on the hallway floor, dropped the pillow on top of it and paced. He was too wound up to sleep and too hard to sit.

Part of him wanted Aurelie to open the door and beg him to come back in, to take her into his arms and screw the rules, screw the truth and screw her.

What he wanted to do warred with what he knew was the right thing to do.

For the love of gumbo, he had sisters. He'd kill a man who took advantage of one of his sisters by leaving out a key piece of information that would help her decide whether he was honorable or a low-life scumbag unworthy of her trust.

Beau wished he hadn't agreed to keep the nature of his assignment a secret from Aurelie. Then again, if she'd known he was a paid employee of her father's, she would have had nothing to do with him other than letting him do his job.

They could have avoided this awkward exchange entirely. She'd have been happy to sleep in his room with him out in the hallway, to begin with. He wouldn't be pacing that hallway with a hard-on so hard he could drive nails with it.

By the twentieth pass going end to end in the hallway, his pulse had almost returned to normal.

Aurelie hadn't opened the door, for which Beau was both thankful and disappointed. It was just as well. His cock was not nearly as hard. He was able to sit on the comforter with his back to the wall without any discomfort, but sleep eluded him until the wee hours of the morning.

He must have nodded off at some point.

The sound of a door's hinges creaking jerked Beau awake. He was on his feet in a flash, his focus on the door behind which Aurelie Anderson slept.

Only the door that opened wasn't his, but another further down the hall, past Romeo's.

Valentin Vachon emerged dressed in a tank top, jogging shorts and running shoes. When he spotted Beau, he frowned. "Lock yourself out?"

Beau shook his head. "On guard duty," he whispered.

Valentin's eyes widened. "I thought I heard something last night."

"Yeah," Beau said. "We came in near midnight."

"I had my noise-canceling earbuds in, listening to white noise. Whoever said living in the country was quiet and peaceful didn't live in southern Louisiana. The damned frogs, crickets and cicadas are every bit as loud as traffic on the LA freeways."

Beau grinned. "True. Good thing I prefer it to traffic."

"I take it you ran into trouble last night."

Beau nodded. "She was attacked at the fundraiser, and her house was ransacked. I had to find a safe place to stash her until I can arrange for a safe house."

Valentin nodded. "I'm headed out for my morning run. I'll keep my eyes peeled."

"Thanks."

"If you need backup, you have my number."

Beau didn't tell his teammate he didn't have a working cell phone. He'd have to remedy that situation soon. "What time is it?"

Valentin checked his watch as he passed Beau in the corridor. "Six-thirty. See ya." The man descended the stairs, quietly exiting the building.

Six-thirty. His mother would be awake by now. She'd know where he could find a place he and Aurelie could hole up in until they got a handle on who was after her. He'd call his mother, but he didn't have a phone that worked.

The metal-on-metal sound of a lock disengaging brought his attention to the door in front of him.

The knob turned, and the door opened.

Aurelie peeked out, her hair in disarray, her face flushed from sleep and sexy as hell. "Hey," she said.

"Hey," he echoed. "Did you get some sleep?"

"Some." She pushed a hand through her thick black hair.

Her movements stretched the T-shirt across her unbound breasts, making Beau want to back her into the room, close the door and weave his hands through the tresses while he made crazy love to her. Keeping his hands off her was going to be one of the toughest tasks he'd ever imagined.

"Hungry?" he asked.

Her gaze met his, her eyelids at half-mast. "Mmm," she murmured, the sound low and gravely.

"I know where we can get a home-cooked breakfast."

She looked down at her outfit and shook her head. "Will they let me through the door dressed like this?"

He grinned. "Absolutely."

"I need to brush my teeth, comb my hair and put

on my boots." She opened the door wider. "You need to use the facilities?"

He nodded. "Thanks."

She stepped aside, allowing him to enter.

"I'd put on the costume I wore last night, but I'm sure it's still wet and smells like the bayou. I rinsed it out when I showered, but it really needs to be thrown in the washing machine with detergent."

"We'll work on getting you something to wear today," he said.

She frowned. "You really don't have to do everything for me. Just because you saved me from drowning doesn't mean you have to be my permanent guardian angel. I can find a way to get back to my car."

"Come to think of it, where is your car?" he asked. "It wasn't at your house."

She shook her head. "No. I met my father at his home in Baton Rouge to help him get ready for the masquerade party. I'd planned on staying the night with him since we'd be getting back so late." Aurelie grimaced. "I'll need to get a driver to take me all the way to Baton Rouge to get my car. I can't keep taking advantage of you."

"You're not." Beau shook his head. "I can't bring myself to walk away from you," he said. "For some reason we don't yet understand, you have a target hanging on your back. I don't feel comfortable abandoning you until we figure out who's gunning for you."

"You wouldn't be abandoning me," she said. "You're not responsible for me. I can take care of myself."

"Obviously," Beau snorted. "When were you planning on coming up for air in the bayou? About the time that alligator reached you?"

Her brow furrowed. "I would've found the surface..." With a dramatic roll of her eyes, she sighed. "Okay. So, I might not have made it out before the alligator got to me. You saved my life, and I probably wouldn't be here arguing with you had you not." She spread her hands out to her sides. "I don't want to be a burden on you. I'm sure you have better things to do with your time—like working or finding a job now that you're out of the military." She paused. "How long have you been out?"

"A couple of years," he answered automatically.

Her brow twisted. "And you haven't found work yet?"

"I went to work for a while in a security firm providing protection for general contractors working in Afghanistan until our country pulled the plug on our presence there."

"Wow." She shook her head. "Isn't that like mercenary work?"

"Some call it that," he admitted. "We were there to protect, not to engage unless we had to."

He edged toward the bathroom, afraid she'd ask more questions, and he'd eventually have to lie or tell her the truth. He'd rather avoid doing either until her father broke it to her that he was being paid to take care of her. "I don't know about you, but I'm hungry. I'm going to shave and change. I'll only be a few minutes, and then you can have the bathroom to yourself."

"Let me grab my things. I can do most everything out here." She ducked into the bathroom and emerged with her bra, her cheeks flushed a soft pink. "All yours."

He nodded, making a mental note to find her some clothes or go by her house after the sheriff's department had dusted for prints. She didn't look like the type of woman who liked running around in public wearing a faded T-shirt and men's shorts, though she looked sexy in them. With her trim figure, long dark hair and deep brown eyes, she'd look good in a paper bag.

He dragged his gaze from her, grabbed a clean pair of jeans from the closet and ducked into the bathroom, silently reminding himself of his responsibility.

She's the job.

Focus.

Beau pulled on the jeans and splashed water on his face and hair. After he combed his hair, he shaved and brushed his teeth and was back out in less than five minutes.

Aurelie sat on the side of the bed, dragging the brush through her hair.

He took the brush out of her hand.

She sighed and turned her back. "My hair is so thick that if I don't have a good conditioner, it takes forever to work out the tangles."

Beau worked through the tangles quickly, afraid if he lingered, he'd end up like he had the previous night, wanting more than to smooth the tangles from her hair. Within a couple of minutes, he finished and handed the brush to her. "We'll find some conditioner for you today."

"Thank you," she said with a smile. "I could get used to having you around."

He'd like to be around under different circumstances, perhaps when he wasn't pretending to be some random guy who'd just happened to save her life.

Aurelie rose from the bed and hurried to the bathroom. "I just have to brush my teeth, and I'll be ready." When her stomach rumbled, she laughed and pressed a hand to her middle. "I guess I'm hungrier than I thought. I look forward to that home-cooked meal."

"Then hurry up. I'm starving." He didn't bother to tell her where they were going for breakfast.

She left the bathroom door open as she

squeezed toothpaste onto a toothbrush and turned on the water in the sink. "I have some at my house. I hope they process for fingerprints early so I can get back in there and assess the damage this morning."

"We can check with the sheriff after breakfast." Beau found a clean black T-shirt in one of his drawers and pulled it over his head, tucking it into the waistband of his jeans. "We also need to get new cell phones. It might mean heading into New Orleans for that." He grabbed socks and found a pair of black combat boots in the closet.

Aurelie emerged from the bathroom as Beau pulled his boots over the socks.

"I hope you don't mind that I borrowed a pair of your socks," she said. "My boots aren't quite dry, but the socks help."

"I'm glad you found some." He pulled on the second boot and stood. "If you need anything else, help yourself or ask, and I'll see if I can find something that will work."

"Do you have a belt I could use?" she asked.

"I do." He reached into the closet and pulled out the two belts he owned. One was brown leather, the other black. "Your choice."

She chose the brown leather and slipped it around her waist, cinching his oversized T-shirt, making it fit like a stylish tunic. The shirt was long enough it almost covered the gym shorts. With the boots she'd worn for her Amelia Earhart costume, she looked like a runway model.

Beau shook his head. "You could wear a paper bag and make it look like a designer piece."

She laughed. "Sometimes, all it takes is accessories. I didn't want to look like a bag lady. I appreciate the T-shirt loaner, but it's so big, I'm almost lost in it." She patted the belt. "This helps tremendously. Thank you for all of it."

"Glad I could help," he said as he slid the black belt through the loops on his jeans and buckled it. "Ready?"

She nodded and walked ahead of him to the door.

"Let me go first." Beau opened the door and stepped out into the hall. When he was certain no one was lurking, waiting to strike, he held out his hand to Aurelie.

She placed her hand in his and allowed him to draw her across the threshold. They left the boarding house, climbed into his truck and headed for breakfast.

When Beau pulled up to a home on the edge of Bayou Mambaloa, Aurelie frowned. "This isn't a restaurant."

He shifted into park. "Did I say I was taking you to a restaurant?"

Her forehead wrinkled as she reluctantly released her seatbelt. "You said you were taking me to breakfast."

"And I am." Beau pushed open his door and dropped to the ground. He rounded the front of the truck as Aurelie slowly opened the door.

He stared up at her. "Are you coming in with me?"

She waved a hand toward the house. "This is someone's home."

"Yes, it is." He reached for her, wrapping his hands around her waist, pulled her from her seat and set her on the ground.

Her frown deepened. "You can't just barge into someone's home without giving them some kind of heads-up."

"Don't worry, I know the cook." He grinned. "She won't mind."

"Even if she's family, you still need to warn her that you're coming and bringing a guest," Aurelie protested as he marched her up the steps of the front porch.

"I couldn't. Remember?" He opened the front door and held it for her. "Our cell phones aren't working."

Aurelie refused to step through the door. "I can't go in uninvited."

Beau shrugged, leaned into the house and shouted, "Hey, Mom, I brought a guest for breakfast!"

A petite woman with sandy-blond hair, much like his, appeared from around a corner. "Beau, honey, is dat you?"

"Yes, ma'am." He took Aurelie's hand and drew

her across the threshold. "This is Aurelie Anderson. We've come for breakfast."

"Perfect," she said with a wide smile. "Come on in. I made plenty of scrambled eggs, pancakes and bacon to go around," she said in her charming Cajun accent. She came forward, wiping her hands on her apron. "Aurelie, so very nice to meet you. I'm Helen Boyette, Beau's *maman*."

As Aurelie shook his mother's hand, she shot a glare at Beau. "Your mother?"

He nodded. "I told you I was taking you to a place where you could get the best breakfast in the parish."

His mother swatted his arm. "Oh, stop." She hooked her arm through Aurelie's. "Come in. Come in. We're in da kitchen, and I'm probably burning something. I love da outfit. You'll have to tell me where you got it. Do you t'ink it would look good on an over-forty-year-old like dis *maman*?"

"I'm sure it would look great on you." Aurelie let Helen lead her away.

"I love da way you accessorized it," his mother said.

Beau followed the two women, shaking his head. His mother didn't know a stranger. Everyone she met was family to her. Their house was where every kid in the parish came to hang out.

The noise level increased with every step as they neared the kitchen.

When Aurelie stepped through the door, it was as if someone had switched off the radio.

For all of a split second.

Then the noise resumed, with everyone talking at once.

"It's a bit loud dis morning." His mother raised her voice to talk above the din. "Dis is Aurelie, Beau's girl."

Aurelie started to shake her head, but Helen Boyette wasn't finished with her introductions. "Sebastian," the older woman said, her forehead wrinkling, "what number are you?"

Beau's brother, dressed in a polo shirt and tan slacks, stepped forward. "Five, *Maman*. Don't you know your own children?"

"*Oui, mon cher*. I changed your diapers like the rest of dem." She patted his cheek and turned to Aurelie. "He's in from Memphis for the weekend." She leaned toward Aurelie and whispered loudly, "He's a big-shot financial advisor dere."

Beau's brother frowned. "*Maman*. I'm not a big-shot." Sebastian held out his hand to Aurelie. "My mother is biased," he said. "Nice to meet you, Aurelie."

Aurelie smiled up at Beau's younger, better-looking brother.

Beau's gut pinched hard. With what?

Jealousy?

He shifted from one foot to the other, studying

Sebastian. When had his little brother become so tall and handsome?

Aurelie looked from Sebastian to Beau. "You look so much alike. You could be twins."

Beau and Sebastian shook their heads.

"No," Sebastian said. "I look nothing like my older brother. My hair is darker like most of my brothers and sisters."

"We're nothing alike," Beau said, though he wished he was a little more like Sebastian and content to work behind a desk. There were so many more jobs for men who didn't mind being in an office all day.

Beau couldn't do it. Thankfully, after the U.S. pulled out of Afghanistan and Beau, with his team of mercenaries, were out of work, Hank Patterson had offered them jobs.

Again, Beau's mother leaned close to Aurelie. "We t'ought maybe da nurses switched babies at da hospital when Beau turned out to be a tow-headed little boy." She grinned. "Den, along came baby Elise, our golden-haired angel. Both children were t'row-backs to my great-grandmother Lanier, an English beauty wit' golden-blond hair." She ruffled Elise's blond curls.

"*Maman*, please." Beau's youngest sister swatted at her mother's hand. She'd been a baby when Beau had joined the Army. He'd done his best to keep in touch with all his siblings when he'd been deployed to other sides of the earth. He'd loved getting Elise's letters, detailing the antics of Jacque, Genevive and Marcel, the kids closest to Elise's age. Now, they were all teenagers.

Where had the time gone?

His mother continued her introductions as she crossed the kitchen and took the spatula from Genevieve's hand. "The boy with the scar across his temple is Theo," Beau's mother said. She dug the spatula into the skillet, moving it around to dislodge the eggs adhering to the metal. "He got that scar swatting at an alligator with his paddle."

"Wow." Aurelie looked at Theo, wide-eyed. "Did the alligator bite you?"

"No," Elise answered for Theo. "He made it mad enough the alligator bumped his pirogue. He flung the paddle in the air and banged his own head with it. All because he wanted to impress Angie Wallace."

Theo laughed. "How do you know all that? You were only five years old when that happened."

Elise rolled her eyes as only a sassy thirteen-year-old could. "I've heard the story so many times I know it by heart." She snorted. "Boys are so stupid when it comes to girls. You were no exception."

Theo held out his hand. "I'm number six."

Aurelie smiled and shook his hand.

Knowing his mother would take forever to introduce the rest of his siblings currently present, Beau took over. He pointed to the sullen, dark-haired nineteen-year-old brother seated at the kitchen table. "Marcel is number seven. He's nineteen and going to diesel mechanic school in Thibodeaux."

Marcel raised a hand. "Hey."

Aurelie nodded. "Hey."

Beau nodded to his pretty seventeen-year-old sister. "That's Genevieve. She's in high school and our most studious sibling, well on her way to becoming the class valedictorian."

Genevieve smiled from her post at the toaster. "Nice to meet you, Aurelie."

Aurelie smiled in return. "Nice to meet you, too."

"The dude manning the waffle iron is my youngest brother, Jacque. Also in high school."

"Not on the fast path to class president," Elise said.

"More likely on the fast path to get a girl pregnant," Marcel murmured.

"Marcel!" Beau's mother held up her spatula. "We have company."

"And what? Don't let her know how we really are when it's just family?" Marcel said. "Shouldn't we be ourselves and let her know what she's getting into if she takes up with Beau?"

His mother glared at him. "You shouldn't be so sassy to anyone. Especially not your family. You're supposed to love family, not pick on dem."

Beau turned to Aurelie. "Just another day in the Boyette family."

She smiled at the people in the kitchen. "It's wonderful. I love that you're all comfortable enough to pick on each other. At least you have each other."

"Do you not pick at your siblings, Aurelie?" Beau's mother asked.

Aurelie shook her head.

"*Maman,*" Beau said. "Aurelie is an only child."

His mother frowned. "An only child? I'm so sorry. Was it lonely growing up?"

Aurelie smiled. "You don't miss what you never had. But I always wished I had a brother or sister."

"And we have enough to share," Elise said.

"Yes, you do," Aurelie said. "You're very fortunate."

Jacque ruffled Elise's hair. "Did you hear that? You're very fortunate to have me as your brother."

Elise slapped at Jacque's hand. "She has no idea how much of a pain it can be havin' multiple siblings."

"*Maman,*" Beau cut through the teasing. "Are you still doing your real estate sales?"

"*Oui, mon cher,*" she said as she scraped the scrambled eggs into a large serving dish. "Why? Are you ready to settle down in your own home?"

"Maybe," Beau hedged. "Miss Anderson needs a place to stay for a day or two where she won't be bothered."

Beau's mother had just lifted the big serving bowl of fluffy-yellow eggs. "I just listed Robbie Pearson's place yesterday."

"I thought Robbie Pearson died," Beau said.

"He did, but he left a fully furnished cottage on de other side of Bayou Mambaloa. His children all live in other cities. They want me to sell da cottage so they can split da proceeds."

"Fully furnished?" Beau asked.

"Yes," his mother said. "Older furniture, quite dated. Da good thing is dat Robbie was meticulous about his home. He kept it clean and neat. Not a lot of personal belongings to sort t'rough." She set the bowl of eggs on the table. "T'inkin' of buyin' a house? You know I'd love to have all my children livin' close."

Beau shook his head, hating the disappointment obvious on his mother's sad frown. "Miss Anderson needs a safe place to stay out of the public eye for a few days to a couple weeks, max."

"If you want somet'ing not too close to other houses and ready to use immediately, Mr. Pearson's home would be da place. I can ask da family members if they'd be willing to rent for a few weeks. Dey might be more willing if you promise to help organize and categorize items for an estate sale or donation to da local women's shelter thrift store."

"I don't mind doing some work to help out," Aurelie said.

"Then I'll call dem now," Beau's mother said with a smile. She laid the platter of scrambled eggs on the table. "Sit. Eat," she ordered and dug her cell phone out of her apron pocket. "Excuse me for a few."

Beau held a chair out for Aurelie.

As she sat, she murmured for his ears only, "I could go stay with my father."

"He's busy campaigning," Beau whispered. "His home would be the next place they'll look to find you."

A moment later, his mother returned to the kitchen. "Robbie's daughter said you can rent by the month for the cost of sortin' t'rough his things and gettin' dem donated." She grinned. "If you need help, I can send Jacque, Genevieve and Elise over."

Aurelie smiled at Beau's mother. "That won't be necessary. I'll do what I can, but I might not be there long."

"Thank you, *Maman*," Beau said. "We'll be sure to leave it clean."

His mother's eyebrows shot up. "You'll be staying dere, too?"

"I assume it has more than one bedroom?" Beau asked.

She nodded. "What about your room at da boarding house?"

"It'll keep. It's just until Aurelie can have some renovations done to her house in Bayou Miste."

His mother's eyes narrowed. "Is dere anything else you want to tell me?"

He stiffened. "No, *Maman*."

"Ha!" Elise said. "Which translates to, *Not with big ears listenin' in.*"

Beau cocked an eyebrow at his little sister. "When did you get to be such a smart Alec?"

"*Maman* said I take after you," she said with a smirk.

Beau grinned, glad he'd come to breakfast at home. They had a safe house.

Now to get Aurelie there and start figuring out who was after her.

CHAPTER 7

DESPITE THE INSTABILITY of her current situation, Aurelie enjoyed breakfast with the Boyette family.

The conversations were lively, ranging from gossip about neighbors in Bayou Mambaloa to the pros and cons of airboats versus pirogues for navigating the bayou's channels. They even discussed the best bait to use fishing off the coast of Louisiana. Aurelie was surprised by how much Beau's mother had to contribute to the conversation about fishing bait.

She learned why soon enough.

Helen smiled across the table at Aurelie. "Are we boring you with talk about fishing?"

"Not at all," Aurelie said.

"Good," Helen said. "Before we had children, I helped Louis on da fishing boat. We went out every day from early in da morning until late in da evening, fishing for shrimp during da shrimp season and everything else in da off-season. Sometimes, we would charter da boat out to wealthy fishermen."

"*Maman's* fishing days weren't over when she had children," Beau said. "There were many times she would pack us all up, along with a lunch, and go out and help my father for the day. She wanted us to understand what our father did."

"Most of my children have not shown an interest in carryin' on deir father's business," Helen said. "Except Pierre. He's out now with Louis. I wouldn't let him join his father on da fishing boat until he got a useful college degree. But he loves fishing and being outdoors. Fortunately, he chose a degree in financial management, which he uses for himself and day trading. He isn't totally reliant on da fishing industry for his income."

"Yeah, Pierre is a lot like me," Beau said. "He doesn't like sitting in an office all day long any more dan I do."

Helen smiled at her son. "Dat's why Beau joined da army."

"But there are many occupations in the army that require sitting behind a desk," Aurelie said.

"My test scores gave me the option to choose a desk job in the army, but that's not what I wanted," Beau said. "I went into the infantry and then applied for Ranger school immediately."

"Rangers are the ones who parachute in?" Aurelie asked.

Beau smiled. "Sometimes. On many occasions, we dropped in by repelling from helicopters. Or we drove into hostile situations in armored personnel carriers. Another option was to go in on foot."

"Army versus civilian life must be so different," Aurelie said.

Beau nodded. "Very different in many ways."

"Was it hard to transition back to civilian life?" Aurelie asked.

"Yes." Beau laid his fork on his plate and looked at his mother. "How soon can we check out Robbie Pearson's house?" He had effectively ended that conversation.

Aurelie suspected he had a reason for not wanting to talk about his time in the army or his transition out. This only made her that much more curious about him.

Helen had finished her breakfast. She collected her plate and pushed back from the table. "I can be ready in five minutes," she said. "I just need to grab my purse and my car keys."

"No hurry," Beau said, but there was no mistaking the tension in him. He collected his plate and Aurelie's and carried them to the sink, where he rinsed them off and placed them in the dishwasher.

"Don't worry about the dishes," Genevieve said.

"We'll take care of them. You go with *Maman*." She smiled at Aurelie. "Nice to meet you."

"If you two move into the Pearson house," Elise said, "can I come visit?"

Helen was halfway out the kitchen door when she paused and looked around at her youngest daughter, a frown denting her forehead. "Now, Elise, don't bother Miss Anderson."

"I won't bother them," Elise said. "It's just that Old Man Pearson's house has a dock on the bayou. It's a great place to swim."

Aurelie blinked. "Aren't you afraid of swimming in the bayou with the alligators?"

Elise grinned. "I enjoy a challenge."

"Elise!" Her mother looked at her with a stern glance.

Elise rolled her eyes. "People up north don't quit going into the woods because of bears. They have a whole campaign on being 'bear aware,'" she said, her eyes narrowed. "We have a similar attitude in the bayou," she said. "We just don't have a cute slogan like *bear aware*. I've been working on it, though." Elise grinned. "What do you think of 'gator radar?'"

Having just had an encounter with an alligator, Aurelie wasn't inclined to use gator radar and tempt the deadly creatures by swimming in the bayou.

Beau directed a narrow-eyed glance at his youngest sister. "I hope you're not swimming in the bayou alone."

Elise gave him an exasperated look. "I'm not *that* dumb. I usually swim with friends, and we are very aware of alligators."

Helen Boyette re-entered the kitchen, carrying her purse and keys. "I'm ready when you are."

Beau dipped his head. "We'll follow you there."

He hooked Aurelie's elbow, and together, they followed his mother out the front door.

Aurelie liked the way his hand felt on her arm, strong but sensitive to her needs. He walked her to the passenger side of his truck and opened the door, waiting for her to climb in before he closed it behind her.

He slid into the driver's seat, started the engine and pulled out behind his mother's graphite-gray SUV. He followed her through town to the opposite end, where the road curved along the shore. She pulled off the public road onto a private driveway leading to a small cottage perched on the bayou's edge.

A plain, white clapboard house with a deep front porch stood in a clearing surrounded by colorful hydrangeas and towering cypress trees. Rocking chairs beckoned visitors to sit and enjoy the morning sunshine. The house reminded Aurelie very much of her little cottage in Bayou Miste.

"It's got good clearance around it," Beau said. "No one can sneak up without coming out into the open.

If you stay here long, I can install some security cameras."

Aurelie shook her head. "I really don't think I'll be here that long."

"You might consider staying here while your cottage is being repainted." Beau pushed open his door and dropped to the ground. He rounded the front of the truck to open her door for her.

Aurelie stared at the cottage, not liking the fact that her own cottage had been violated. She itched to get back inside of it and clean up the mess that had been made. "I'll probably do my own painting," she said, thinking out loud. "It was on my list of things to do after I bought the house. I just hadn't gotten around to it yet."

"You might hold off painting until you know for sure who did the damage," Beau suggested. "You don't want to paint and have them come behind you and damage it all over again."

Aurelie's lips pressed into a tight line. "Why do people have to be such assholes?"

Beau chuckled. "I don't know. Hopefully, whoever is causing you grief won't find you anytime soon here in Bayou Mambaloa."

Helen Boyette ascended the steps ahead of them and worked the combination on the lockbox hanging on the doorknob. Once open, she extracted the key from inside and handed the key to Beau. "I'll let you do da honors. I've already seen da inside."

Beau fit the key into the lock, twisted and then pushed open the door. He stepped back and allowed Aurelie to enter first.

As she stepped across the threshold, she was met with the same musty smell she'd encountered when she'd first walked into her cottage. She'd purchased her house from an 80-year-old woman who'd decided to move in with her daughter in Atlanta. This home, like hers, had to be between seventy and eighty years old and just needed a little TLC to brighten it up to date. And like Helen had said, the furniture was dated but in surprisingly good shape.

Helen flipped a light switch, and an overhead light blinked on. "Dey left the utilities on, so you should have water and electricity. I know dere's a washer and dryer in the laundry room, and Mr. Pearson had a dishwasher installed in da kitchen a couple o' years ago."

"That will be nice," Aurelie said. At least she wouldn't have to find a laundromat to do her laundry. Again, she didn't plan on staying there long. Hopefully, the sheriff would have some news for them soon regarding who had attacked her at the château. She was interested in seeing the video footage they would be reviewing from the cameras posted around the exterior of the château.

In the meantime, she had to come up with more clothes to wear besides her costume and Beau's boxer briefs. Hopefully, she could get into her house soon to see whether she could salvage her clothing.

Helen walked with them through the house, pointing out the different things that needed to be sorted and either donated to a thrift store or taken to the dump. "You might set all da photographs and any jewelry or memorabilia aside for da family to go t'rough. But dey didn't want to keep his clothing, bedding or furniture for dat matter."

"I do have a day job," Aurelie said. "But I'll do what I can in the evenings. Please thank the Pearsons for their hospitality."

"I will," Helen said. "Now, if you'll excuse me, I have a showing of a business on Main Street I need ta get to get ready for."

"Thank you, *Maman*." Beau kissed his mother's cheek. "I knew you could help."

His mother stared up into his eyes. "Now that the other children are not around, perhaps you can tell me what's going on...?"

Beau lifted his chin toward Aurelie. "Miss Anderson was attacked at the château last night, and her house in Bayou Miste was ransacked." He held out his hand toward Aurelie.

She placed her palm in his. "What your son is not saying is that he rescued me from the bayou and now feels responsible for me."

Helen Boyette smiled. "He's a good man like his

father." She patted him on his arm. "I'm sorry to hear about da attack, and I'm glad you're OK. Stick with Beau. He'll take good care of you."

Beau's lips twisted. "Thanks for the vote confidence."

"You can pay me back by cleaning the gutters on my house dis coming weekend," his mother said with a grin. She winked at Aurelie. "Be careful. If you need anything, you know where I live."

Helen left the cottage, climbed into her SUV and drove to her next showing.

Aurelie stood in the middle of the little living room with the floral couch bearing shades of burnt orange and brown and said, "It's really nice of your mother to find this for me. But I'd much rather be in my own place."

"Like you said, it shouldn't be for long." He entered the kitchen and pulled open the refrigerator. It was empty. "You'll need a few groceries to last a couple of days at least. Can you cook?"

Aurelie chuckled. "Most things I burn. Even water."

Beau shot a glance her way, his eyebrows rising up his forehead. "You burn water?"

Aurelie grimaced. "I was actually boiling water and forgot that I was boiling water."

He shook his head. "All the water burned out of the pan, right?".

"Pretty much." She entered the kitchen with him and opened what appeared to be a pantry door. Inside were a few cans of soup and several canisters labeled flour, sugar, cornmeal, and coffee. Half a bag of dog food lay on the floor.

Aurelie frowned. "I wonder what happened to Mr. Pearson's dog. Do you think it passed before he did? And if not, did the family take it? Or did they dump it at a shelter?"

Beau lifted the bag of dog food. "I'd like to think the family adopted it."

Aurelie pointed to the half of a bag of dog food. "If they took the dog, why didn't they take the dog's food?"

"Good question. I'll ask my mother to check with the family." He met her gaze. "Now that we have established a place for you to stay, let's see about getting our phones restored."

Aurelie nodded. "You don't realize how much we rely on our phones until we don't have them. Like, I feel naked without mine." Her lips twisted. "And at the same time, I feel free. Since last night, I haven't received a single death threat."

Beau escorted her to the door. "Do you want to keep the key, or do you want me to hold onto it?"

"You are insisting on accompanying me every-where and staying at the cottage; you might as well keep the key," Aurelie said. "That way, when I can go back to my own cottage, you can return the key to your mother."

"Fair enough," Beau said. "I'd suggest going to a smaller town, but we'll probably have a better selection and quicker service if we go into New Orleans to get the phones."

"Agreed," Aurelie said. "I need to check in with my father. My abrupt departure from the masquerade ball last night probably has him worried."

"Then, New Orleans it is." He locked the door behind them and walked with her out to the truck.

Aurelie looked around the cottage and out toward the bayou. "This is a nice place," she said. "It just needs some updating. How many acres did your mother say came with the house?"

"I think she said ten acres." He glanced around. "If you don't mind, I'd like to look behind the house. It'll only take a second."

"I'd like to as well," she said and followed him as he rounded the outside of the building.

The back of the house had another wide deck with a porch swing hanging on either end. A stone walkway led down to a dock with a small boat tied to one side. The dock appeared to be in fairly good condition, if slightly weathered.

"Mr. Pearson must've had the dock reworked in the last few years," Beau said. "I wonder how Elise knew about it. I suspect my young sister is a bit of an adventurer and finds her way around the bayou."

"I like her." Aurelie smiled. "She appears to be full of grit and sass."

"Sass is a given when it comes to Boyettes." Beau grinned. "I hope I get to know her better now that I'm back home. I joined the army when she was little. So, I missed out on most of her life."

"Like you said, now that you're back, you can make up for lost time."

Beau nodded. "If she lets me in. After all, she's a teenager."

"You are very fortunate to have so many siblings."

"I didn't think so growing up," he said. "Peace and quiet were not in our cards. But it was nice to know they were there for my folks when I left. There'll always be somebody here to help my mother and father." He glanced her way. "Ready?"

"I am." Aurelie walked with him back to the truck and climbed in.

Soon, they were on their way to New Orleans. Traffic wasn't bad, and they made it to the cell phone store in under an hour. Fortunately, the store was able to set them both up with new cell phones and transfer all their data.

As soon as Aurelie's cell phone was up and running with the old phone number, multiple texts came through, and she had several voice messages. She started with the voice messages. Three of them were from her father, who was worried that she wasn't answering her phone. He wanted an update.

While Aurelie checked her messages, Beau listened to his. After one message, he turned and walked a few steps away from her to place a call. He spoke softly into the phone, where she couldn't make out his words or who he was talking to.

Aurelie chose that moment to respond to her father's voicemails using the callback number. His phone didn't ring but went straight to voicemail. He was probably on the line with someone else. She left a brief message telling him she was fine and that she'd call him again soon.

She dreaded looking at her text messages. After all that had happened, she knew for sure there would be more from her tormentor. She drew a deep breath and touched the icon for her text messages. Three of them were from her father, demanding she call back immediately. Two of them were from the contact she'd been using to get information about a certain corporation that was suspected of dumping toxins into the Bayou. The last text message was the one that made her gut knot.

YOU SHOULD BE DEAD

Her pulse quickened. Heat rushed up her neck into her cheeks. "Bastard!"

"What's wrong?" Beau appeared at her side.

She held up her cell phone with the text message.

"Bastard," Beau said.

Aurelie chuckled. "My thoughts exactly. Are you all caught up?"

"I am," he said.

"I'd like to head back to Bayou Miste," Aurelie said. "We can stop by the sheriff's office for an update on the damage done to my house. Hopefully, he can find out if the sheriff near Gautreaux Château made any headway through the video footage from the security cameras."

"I have a friend with connections in law enforcement," Beau said. "I can have him check on the sheriff's office that's looking at the video footage from the château. That way, we can focus on Bayou Miste and the damage done to your house."

"Sounds good," Aurelie said. "I'd like to get a change of clothes. As hip as I am in this outfit, I'll need some things for the next few days, including conditioner for my hair."

"Okay," he said as they walked out of the parking lot to his truck.

After she settled into the passenger seat, she waited for Beau to get in. "Do you mind if I call my father?"

"Not at all." He started the truck engine and drove out of the parking lot, heading west of New Orleans.

Aurelie called her father and waited as it rang.

He answered on the second ring. "Sweetie, are you okay?"

"I'm fine, Dad." She wondered how much he knew about what had happened the night before. She didn't want him to get upset.

"I can't believe you didn't tell me about the attacks," her father railed.

Aurelie sighed. So much for him not knowing. "I didn't want to disturb your fundraising event," she said. "Who told you about the attacks?"

"I have my sources," her father said. "The point is that you aren't safe. You need to move back home."

Aurelie shook her head. "I don't need to move back home. I need to make a life of my own."

"Well then, you need a bodyguard 24/7," her father said.

"I kind of have one," Aurelie said. "He might not want to be, but he's insisting."

"Is he that guy you were dancing with last night?" her father asked.

"Yes, sir." As usual, he'd been watching her. Her father would never stop worrying about his only daughter.

"Is he taking care of my little girl?"

Aurelie frowned. "Dad, you have to stop calling me a little girl. I am a grown woman."

Her father snorted. "You might be a grown woman to everyone else, but to me, you'll always be my little girl."

She couldn't argue with the man and didn't want to. "All you need to know is that I'm okay. I have someone looking out for me."

"You tell Beau to take care of my little girl."

"I'll do no such thing," she said. "I love you, Dad."

"I love you, too," he said softly. "You're all I have."

"Bye, Dad." She ended the call, frowning. "My father knew about both attacks. The one in the bayou and the one at my house." She glanced toward Beau. "How the hell did he get information about the one at my house?"

Beau raised both eyebrows and glanced her way. "You should've asked him."

"Yeah," Aurelie said, "I should have. Sometimes, that man knows more about my business than I do. You'd think he had someone spying on me at all times."

Beau didn't respond, his attention on the road in front of him.

Aurelie knew her dad loved her and only wanted the best for her. After losing his wife in an accident and almost losing his daughter, he could be overly cautious. She couldn't blame him. Her father was her only family. She'd be devastated if something happened to him.

"Have you always worked for your father?" Beau asked.

"No," Aurelie said. "I lived and worked in Memphis for a year after I graduated from college with a degree in marketing."

"Why did you leave Memphis?"

She glanced out the side window. "I got into a relationship with a guy I thought I knew. Then I found out I didn't know him at all. He was married and didn't bother telling me."

"That sucks," Beau said. "How did you find out?"

She gave a brief, humorless laugh. "I expected him for dinner one night. I'd roasted my first chicken, made scalloped potatoes, broccoli and cheese casserole and set the table with wine and candles. When I opened my apartment door, a pretty blonde stood there. She introduced herself as his wife. She showed me photographs of their children."

Beau winced. "Ouch."

"No kidding." Aurelie stared down at his hands. "I was shocked. I was young and stupid. I never considered he might be married. Married guys aren't supposed to ask a girl out who isn't his wife."

"Sounds like a real jerk."

"He was. The problem was that I worked with the guy. I promised never to see him again, which was a no-brainer. But I saw him every day in the hallways. I was so angry that it was affecting my work. After a week of trying to avoid him, I turned in my resignation, tucked my tail between my legs and moved back to Baton Rouge to look for work. I wasn't finding much of anything for someone with only a year's experience."

"In Baton Rouge? What about New Orleans?"

She shook her head. "I couldn't find work in either place. Then, the woman who'd been in charge of my dad's philanthropy project announced that she was pregnant and wanted to be a stay-at-home mom. She handed in her resignation. My father offered me the position. I took him up on it."

"The project to save the bayou?" Beau asked.

Aurelie nodded. "It was supposed to be an advertising campaign to save the bayou. We would educate the public and work with the Environmental Protection Agency to ensure companies were doing right by the bayou. I didn't see the companies doing right. I got tips from insiders telling me some companies were ignoring regulations and allowing toxins to seep into the bayou. I sort of became the bayou police, though that was not my intention." She gave him a weak smile. "Anyway, that's how I ended up working for my father. All because of a man."

"The guy was a jerk," Beau said. "He didn't deserve you. For that matter, he didn't deserve his wife."

"Oh, I agree with you one hundred percent. If I were a more vindictive person with a violent streak, I would've cut off his balls. That would be the only way to keep him from screwing the next woman because you know that if he cheated on his wife once, he'll do it again."

Beau nodded. "Remind me not to piss you off, especially if you're anywhere near a knife."

She laughed. "Don't worry, I'm not the violent type. Though the thought did cross my mind."

Beau pulled into the sheriff's office parking lot and shifted into park.

Aurelie didn't wait for him to open the door for her. Instead, she met him at the front of the truck. They walked into the sheriff's office together.

The sheriff emerged from a door behind the reception desk. "I'm glad you came in this morning." The sheriff held out his hand to Aurelie. "They finished lifting prints earlier this morning. We've already isolated yours. We got a good set of prints off the bedroom doorknob. We're running it through the Integrated Automated Fingerprint Identification System. If this guy has had his fingerprints processed before, we should be able to find a match."

"Is it okay for me to go back to my house?" Aurelie asked.

The sheriff nodded. "We've done all the evidence gathering we can. Since the suspect is still at large, be careful. He might come back. I'd change the locks before you stay there for any length of time."

"I'll be careful," Aurelie said. "You'll let me know if you find anything?"

"Yes, ma'am," the sheriff said. "And I'll let the senator know as well."

Aurelie's brow dipped. "Has he been in touch?"

"Yes, ma'am," the sheriff said. "He was worried about you—and we're checking to see if this attack has anything to do with the attack at the Gautreaux Château. We'll be working closely with the sheriff of that parish."

"Thank you." Aurelie turned to Beau. "Let's go."

She walked out to the truck, her thoughts spinning. "I really hope they find a match on that fingerprint. Because I have no clue who's after me, and it's bugging the crap out of me."

"Same," Beau said. "Makes you wonder if the same guy who attacked you at the château came here to destroy your home?"

"I had that thought as well." Aurelie climbed into the truck and buckled her seatbelt.

Beau got in and started the engine.

"We went from the château to the parish sheriff's office before coming to Bayou Miste. Would that have given him enough time to do all the damage he did?" she asked.

"It probably gave him a thirty to forty-five-minute lead on us." Beau rested his hand on the gear shift. "You would think the paint on the wall might still be wet. I touched it. It was dry. Your point?" Beau cocked an eyebrow.

"It's bad enough if I have one person chasing after me." A shiver rippled down Aurelie's spine. "Lord help me if there's more."

They drove the short distance from the sheriff's office to Aurelie's cottage. She sat for a moment, staring at the place she'd so lovingly decorated over the past several weeks since she'd moved in. "It doesn't feel right anymore."

"It probably won't for a while." Beau stared at her cottage. "In effect, your house has been violated."

That was exactly how she felt.

Violated.

A shiver rippled down her spine.

She refused to let some bastard scare her away from everything she'd worked so hard for. Aurelie squared her shoulders.

CHAPTER 8

"Well," Beau said, "let's go in, get a few of your things and then head back to Bayou Mambaloa."

Aurelie took a deep breath. "Okay. I'm feeling better about the little house in Bayou Mambaloa. It might take me a little while before I feel safe in my own home again."

Beau dropped down out of his pickup and came around to open the door for Aurelie. He held out his hand to her.

Aurelie had always considered herself an independent woman, but she was glad Beau had come along when he had. She wasn't sure what she would've done had he not. She probably would've drowned in the bayou or gotten eaten by an alligator. She let him help her down from the truck to stand in front of him on the ground. For a moment, she stared up into his handsome face, marveling again at how blue his eyes were. She'd been entranced by them at the masquerade ball. That had to be why she'd let him kiss her on the dance floor.

The memory of that kiss made heat rise up her neck into her cheeks. Aurelie ducked her head and turned toward the house.

Beau cupped her elbow, fanning the flames as he walked with her to her house.

The heat chilled as she climbed the steps onto the porch.

She'd been there the night before, but it felt like she hadn't been there for a long time. Aurelie pulled the front door key out of her pocket and handed it to Beau. "If you don't mind."

"I don't mind," Beau said. "Like the sheriff said, you'll need to get new locks installed before you move back in."

"And a security system," Aurelie added.

"That would be a good idea," Beau said

He unlocked the door and pushed it open. "Let me go first."

Aurelie had no problem with letting Beau enter first. A burglar would be stupid to lie in wait inside a house under investigation by law enforcement. But then, whoever was after her had not been deterred by a château full of guests.

Beau entered her home, leaving the door wide open. Aurelie could see him moving around as he checked in the kitchen, the living room and then disappeared into the hallway leading to the bedrooms.

Moments later, he returned and said, "All clear."

Aurelie crossed the threshold into her home with a sad, sick feeling in her belly. She'd seen it the night before, but in the cold light of day, it still hit her in the gut.

Beau gripped her elbow. "Let's get your things and get out of here."

She nodded, squared her shoulders, and marched down the hallway to the master bedroom, refusing to look at the trashed living room.

She hadn't gotten that far the night before. Her bedroom was as much of a disaster as the rest of her house. The dresser drawers had been yanked out, and the clothes inside had been flung across the room. Her bed, which she had taken pride in making every morning with its beautiful comforter, was a shambles. The comforter had been ripped as if somebody had jabbed a knife into it and flung it across the room. Like the comforter, the sheets had been ripped down the middle. Even the mattress had a big tear down the center. Aurelie pressed a hand to her chest. Had she been lying in that bed when the intruder had slashed the mattress, would he have slashed through her as well?

Beau laid a hand on her shoulder. "Focus on getting the clothes you need."

Aurelie swallowed hard, nodded and stepped over the mess.

Beau walked towards the closet and grabbed a gym bag that had been thrown on the floor. He unzipped it and laid it down next to Aurelie's feet.

Not wanting to stay there any longer than she had to, Aurelie picked through the clothes on the floor and shoved underwear, bras, shirts and jeans into the gym bag. Though her natural inclination was to set everything to rights, the mess was so big she couldn't fathom where to begin. Once the bag was full, she grabbed a pair of tennis shoes, a nice pair of heels and a couple of dresses that had been thrown out of her closet. She jammed them into the bag and zipped it closed.

"Toiletries?" Beau prompted. "How about that conditioner?" he said with a smile.

Aurelie entered the bathroom, her heart sinking to the very pit of her belly. The mirror over the sink had been smashed, and more spray paint had been splashed across the wall, which had the same message as in the living room.

DIE BITCH!

She tried not to fixate on the message and looked around for her shampoo and conditioner.

The bottles had been upended and emptied across the floor, making it a slippery nightmare. Her makeup, brushes, curling iron and blow dryer lay in the gooey, sticky mess.

Aurelie backed out of the bathroom, shaking her head. "I just can't."

"Come on, babe." Beau took her hand. "Let's go. We can shop for what you need. The store in Bayou Mambaloa might not have exactly what you need, but they should have enough that you can get by until we make another trip to New Orleans." He led her out of the bathroom, grabbed the gym bag and kept her moving toward the exit.

Too sick at heart to do anything else, Aurelie left her bedroom. On her way back through the house, she paused to scoop up a fuzzy pillow that hadn't been destroyed and plucked the photograph of her family off the floor. She hugged them against her chest and gave one last look around before turning away. "I'm done," she said and walked out the front door.

Beau closed and locked the door behind them.

Why he should bother locking the door, Aurelie didn't know. The intruder had her key. He could come back whenever he wanted and waltz right in.

"I need to call a handyman to have those new locks installed," she said.

Beau carried her gym bag to the truck and tossed it onto the backseat. He took the items she had in her hands and laid them on the backseat alongside the gym bag.

Aurelie climbed into the truck as if in a trance, struggling to maintain perspective. It could have been so much worse if she had been at her home when the intruder had invaded. He could have burned the house to the ground.

"Things can be replaced," Beau said as he got into the truck beside her.

"True," she said. The violence of the attack at the château and inside her house worried her.

She wondered how long it would take for her attacker to find her in Bayou Mambaloa. She hoped not soon. In the meantime, she had Beau. She glanced over the console at the man who'd saved her in the bayou like some guardian angel, who'd appeared when she'd needed him most. How lucky she was he'd come along when he had?

BEAU DIDN'T LIKE the idea that he couldn't tell Aurelie that her father had hired him. It tied his hands and made his job even harder. He needed to make phone calls to his team to get them working on background checks on the people in Aurelie's life. Beau sat for a moment, tapping his fingers against the steering wheel.

"What are you thinking?" Aurelie asked.

"I'm thinking I need to get my cousins to keep an eye on your place," Beau said. "If you don't mind, I'd like to make a stop."

"Please," she said. "I'd appreciate any help I can get."

"Have you been to Thibodeaux Marina?" Beau asked.

Aurelie shook her head. "I haven't had that much time to get around to all the places in Bayou Miste. The only people I've really met are Ben, Lucy, Alex and Ed. I'm very involved in my father's philanthropy, so I'm on the road a lot. I've been to the general store in town a couple of times and wandered through a festival, but I've always been in a hurry. I guess I need to slow down long enough to meet more of my neighbors." She grimaced. "I had all good intentions of doing that after the masquerade party."

"Well, when this is over, I'll introduce you to the rest of the clan." Beau turned off the main road and drove down a side street. "For now, I need to speak with my cousin Ben."

"How does he fit in the Bayou Miste hierarchy?" she asked.

Beau grinned. "He's number one of nineteen."

Aurelie's brow wrinkled. "And Alexandra?"

"Number two," Beau said. "Ben married Lucy, the granddaughter of Bayou Miste's infamous voodoo queen. Lucy is a sweetheart. She has a twin sister named Lisa. You might want to avoid that one. She's been known to cause trouble. Although, I think I heard them say something about her having moved to Atlanta. Aunt Barbara said all of Bayou Miste breathed a sigh of relief when she left."

"Why?"

"She stirred up trouble everywhere she went," he said. "They were afraid she'd learn too much from her voodoo queen grandmother and turn everyone into toads or mushrooms."

"Do you believe in all that voodoo stuff?" Aurelie asked.

"I keep an open mind," Beau said. "I've heard of strange things happening in Bayou Miste. Things that can't be explained away by science."

Aurelie's eyebrows twisted. "Like what?"

"My cousin Alexandra swears that Lucy gave her a potion bag that made her dog turn into a man."

Aurelie eyebrows rose on her forehead. "She seriously believed that?"

Beau raised the hand. "She swears by it—and so does her friend Calliope. I can't vouch for it. I was deployed to Iraq at the time that happened."

Aurelie gave him a skeptical look. "I don't know whether to be intrigued or a little leery of meeting the rest of your cousins in Bayou Miste."

Beau laughed. "They're harmless. A little kookie, but harmless."

"I'll take your word for it."

"Well, you've met Ben."

"Yes," Aurelie said. "He's pretty normal from what I've seen."

"He says that Lucy tried to put a love spell on him once. He also said he would've believed it worked, except he's always been in love with her, even before she said she cast her love spell."

Aurelie laughed. "I think I'm going to go with intrigued. Your cousins sound interesting. I look forward to meeting the rest of them."

"I always liked coming over to Bayou Miste to visit," Beau said. "We had grand adventures. I remember one time, as young teens, we snuck into Charlie Hughes's watermelon patch. I almost got an ass full of buckshot for the effort."

Aurelie chuckled. "I can picture a younger version of you sneaking into a watermelon patch."

Beau cocked one eyebrow and glanced her way. "Oh, you can, can you?"

"I can imagine your hair being a little bit lighter blond and maybe your shoulders weren't quite as broad. But I can imagine that smirky grin on your face. So, did Charlie Hughes tell your cousins' mother what you all had been up to?"

"Sadly, yes," he said. "It's a small town. You can't get away with much. Secrets can be hard to keep."

"Were you all punished?" she asked.

Beau nodded. "She could've had us all go pick our own switch for an old-fashioned spanking. Instead, she had us go back to Charlie Hughes's farm and help pull weeds in the watermelon patch. We had to spend the entire day pulling weeds while our friends went swimming."

"That had to hurt," Aurelie said with a grin.

"It did," Beau said. "But Charlie Hughes worked alongside us. He didn't say much, but he did tell us enough about raising watermelons, how to plant them and how to tell when they were ripe. Because you see, the watermelon we tried to steal was green. At the end of the day, he had each of us pick a ripe watermelon. He sent us home with the melon."

Aurelie smiled. "What a nice thing for him to do."

"After the watermelon patch incident, whenever I visited, we all went over to Charlie Hughes's and helped him weed his watermelon patch. Sometimes, it was the corn patch or the cantaloupes. Then we'd sit with him on the porch at the back of his house and eat the fruits of our labors. He told us stories of when he was a teenager and got caught stealing watermelon from his neighbor's watermelon patch. Only his neighbor wasn't nearly as nice. He'd vowed to handle it differently if it ever happened to him. So, in a way, he was kind of glad to have the opportunity to do it right."

"I kind of love that story." Aurelie stared out the window as they drove into Bayou Miste. "I think I'm going to like this town."

"It is a pretty great place to live," he said. "Bayou Mambaloa is very much like it. In towns like this, people look out for each other, for the most part."

He pulled into the parking lot at Thibodeaux's Marina.

"Does your cousin Benjamin work here?" Aurelie asked.

"On Sundays, he likes to work with Joe Thibodeaux, the man who owns the marina," Beau said. "If he's not here, we'll swing by his house."

Beau got out of the truck. Aurelie met him at the front, and they walked together down to the marina and into the building, which had signs posted outside advertising bait and fishing gear for sale.

As he entered the building, Beau stood just inside the door, allowing his eyes to adjust to the dim lighting.

"Beau Boyette, is that you?" a voice boomed. Benjamin Boyette came out from behind the counter at the far end of the store, wearing a baseball cap and a T-shirt with a faded Led Zeppelin logo scrawled across it. "Man, is it good to see you." He wrapped his arms around Beau and hugged him so tightly Beau could barely breathe.

Beau hugged his cousin back just as hard. His heart swelled, and his eyes misted. He hadn't realized how much he'd missed his cousin, his family and his home. More than that, he missed the innocence and simplicity of the life he'd had growing up. Seeing Ben brought it all back. But home wasn't the same. No. Beau wasn't the same.

Benjamin clapped him on the back several times, pushed him to arm's length and stared into his face. "How are you?"

Beau dipped his head. "Good. I see some things never change. You're still helping out here at the marina…?"

Benjamin nodded. "I'm trying to get Joe to bring the place into the twenty-first century. He did get several new bass boats for his boat rental business."

"I'll have to check them out," Beau said.

"He had to do it since the old ones were disappearing."

"Disappearing?" Beau gave Benjamin a quizzical look.

"Strangers would rent them and never bring them back." Beau's cousin shook his head. "They'd give what appeared to be real driver's licenses, use a credit card and then poof!" He waved his hand as if casting a magic spell. "The men and boats left and never returned. We suspect they were running drugs through the bayou."

"Damn. And Joe's replacing them?" Beau's brow wrinkled. "Why?"

His cousin grinned. "I came up with a plan to put a stop to asset loss."

"How did you do that?" Beau asked.

"I attached a tracking device to each boat. The tracking application keeps tabs on where it goes and shows the path it took. You can count on the tracker to display exactly where the boat is at any given time." He grinned. "Just a week ago, we had one of those rent-and-run situations. When the man didn't bring the boat back by closing time, we brought up the application, closed the marina and took another boat out to find the missing one."

"Did you find it?" Beau asked.

Benjamin grinned. "We did. It had been abandoned beneath a cypress tree with branches that bent low enough to dip into the water. People just passing by in other watercraft wouldn't be able to see the abandoned boat behind the veil of cypress branches. We recovered the new boat and have been renting it out since with no problem."

"Do you tell your clients that you're recording their routes?" Aurelie asked.

"Joe and I talked about being transparent with our customers and decided it wasn't worth scaring them away from renting boats at the marina again. Most people who rent are good people looking to have a great day boating or fishing. The trackers are for the dirtbags stealing the boats. We want the good people back to generate more income."

Beau pounded his cousin's back. "Glad it's working out for you."

"Enough about boats...How the hell are you?" Benjamin's brow formed a V over his nose. "We heard about the crash. We were so glad you survived." Ben hugged him again.

Beau didn't respond. Mention of the crash only resurrected that hard lump in his throat whenever he thought about his team. The men who had been his brothers were now gone. Kemper, Wykowski, Jones, Cortez, Martin, Cooley and Biggs. The men he'd fought alongside. The guys with whom he'd shared meals, drinks, training exercises and missions. All gone. Everyone but Beau had died in that helicopter crash. The heavy weight of loss threatened to overwhelm Beau. He couldn't let it. He drew in a deep breath and let it out.

Ben stared into his eyes. "I'm so sorry about your team. I know they had to have meant a lot to you. But we're glad you're home." Ben dropped his arms to his side. "So, how's the new job?"

Ben's question brought Beau back to the present and what he needed to focus on. "It's good." He turned to Aurelie, eager to move Ben away from questioning him more about his job, thus cluing Aurelie into the fact that he was her bodyguard. "Ben, I believe you've met Aurelie."

Ben held out his hand to Aurelie. "Yes, we met at the Raccoon Saloon. You bought the old Dupree place on the edge of town."

Aurelie nodded and shook Ben's hand. "That's me," she said. "I moved in several weeks ago. I just haven't had time to get around and meet all the residents of Bayou Miste. I was glad to meet you, Alex and your spouses."

"Don't worry. You'll meet the rest of the crew all too soon," Ben said. "People around here have a way of getting all up in your business. Before long, you'll know everyone."

Aurelie grinned. "I look forward to that. And it's nice to meet you. Lucy was very welcoming when she came over the other day and brought me the talisman to keep me safe."

Ben's brow wrinkled. "I'd be careful with whatever Lucy cooks up. You never know what it is or what it's going to do. That Voodoo hoodoo stuff can get a little dicey at times."

"How's she doing?" Beau asked.

"She's doing great," Ben said with a smile. "She's been working with her grandmother on natural remedies. She's learned a lot and has opened up a shop in town. It's been a pretty cool tourist attraction. The shop carries homemade candles, incense, voodoo dolls and the natural remedies that her grandmother has shown her how to make out of plants and herbs you can find in the bayou. It's pretty popular with the tourists and with the locals. So popular, she's making decent money—and it keeps her too busy to meddle with casting spells." He frowned. "At least, I think it does."

"Sounds great," Beau said. "I'm glad she's making a name for herself and found her calling."

"She's about to get even busier." Ben's grin widened. "We're expecting a baby."

Beau pulled his cousin in for another hug, clapping him on the back. "That's great news. I can't believe you're going to be a father."

Ben blinked. "I know. I'm still trying to get used to the idea."

"If you have a boy, will you let him run wild in the bayou like we did?" Beau asked.

Ben's eyes widened. "Actually, I'm a bit terrified. What if he turns out to be just like me? I won't be able to hold him back."

Beau laughed. "That is something to be terrified about. We did get into a lot of trouble. I'm surprised we lived through our teen years."

"Exactly." Ben frowned. "I barely lived through childhood. How can I keep a mini-me alive to adulthood?"

"I'm sure you'll do great as a father," Beau said. "Congratulations."

"Thanks. I hope you're right." Ben looked from Beau to Aurelie. "Did you come to Bayou Miste just to visit me, or can I help you with something?"

Beau's smile faded. "I don't know if you heard the news, but Aurelie's place was broken into last night."

Ben's eyebrows rose. "I hadn't heard that. I'm sorry." He stared at Aurelie. "Are you all right?"

Aurelie nodded. "I wasn't there at the time."

"We were at the masquerade ball at Gautreaux Château," Beau said. "Her father, Senator Anderson, is running for reelection. They were having a fundraiser at the château. Aurelie was attacked on the bayou boardwalk outside the château."

"Holy shit," Ben exclaimed. "What the hell?"

Beau continued, "She's had several death threats over the last few days. So, she's kind of hanging with me until they figure out who's behind them. She won't be staying at her place until they determine who's responsible."

"Wow," Ben said. "I'm sorry to hear that. I hope they figure it out quickly. What can I do for you in the meantime?"

Aurelie glanced toward Beau.

He held out his hand. She placed hers in his.

"If you could keep an eye on her place every once in a while, that would help," Beau said. "If you see anybody suspicious hanging around town, get a license plate or something. Let me know. Until we figure out who is behind the threats, she'll stay elsewhere with me. You have my number. Call me if you notice anything or anyone acting strangely."

"Will do." Ben nodded. "I'll let the family know to keep an eye out, as well."

Beau grinned. "Nineteen pairs of eyes. Make that twenty, counting your mom. That should help."

"Speaking of mom," Ben said. "She'll want to know when you're coming to dinner."

"Tell her I'll be by when things settle down," Beau said. "How is she?"

Ben's lips twisted. "Working on her next project."

ELLE JAMES

"And which one of your siblings is she trying to match now?" Beau said with a grin.

Ben shook his head. "She's set on finding matches for Harry and Truman. They're ready to move to the other side of the world to avoid that nonsense."

Beau laughed. "Why are they so worried? Didn't she find Alexandra a husband?"

"She did." Ben's lips twisted. "That's the problem. Now, she thinks she's got the corner on the market of matchmaking. She's not satisfied to just concentrate on her own children, she's been helping some of the other young singles in Bayou Miste. I heard she's working on Alexandra's friend Calliope."

Beau shook his head. "I've been gone way too long," he said. "To me, Alexandra and Calliope are still the little girls with pigtails, following around behind us when we went on our adventures. I have to admit I can't see Alexandra allowing your mother to find a match for her."

"Oh, she resisted." Ben snorted. "But damned if Ed isn't perfect for her. They found a place halfway between Morgan City and Baton Rouge, so that they didn't have to give up their jobs."

Beau tilted his head. "Does Alex still have her gym?"

Ben nodded. "And her husband, Ed, works with the Criminal Investigations Division of the Louisiana State Police Department."

"I bet he's got some stories to tell," Beau said.

"They never would've met had he not been here protecting a witness that he hid out in the bayou to keep her safe so that she could testify against a mobster."

"Sounds like a good guy." Beau smiled. "I'm glad Alexandra found someone to love."

Ben nodded. "Yeah. Someone who values her independence and stubborn streak. They are perfect for each other."

"And I'm happy to see that you and Lucy are back together," Beau said. "You were so tight when we were teens. I'm glad you worked things out between the two of you."

"Me too," Ben said. "Life is never boring with Lucy around." He turned to Aurelie. "I look forward to getting to know you better. Lucy had good things to say about you after her visit."

Aurelie smiled. "It was very nice of her to welcome me. Hopefully, this drama will settle down, and I can spend more time getting to know my neighbors in Bayou Miste."

"It will," Beau said. "For now, we're heading out."

Ben walked with them to the door. "Let me know when you're ready for a little fishing or frog gigging."

"Ew." Aurelie grimaced. "Leave me out of that invite."

Ben laughed. "I will." He waved from the door as Bean and Aurelie walked out to the truck.

Beau opened the passenger side door and helped

Aurelie up into her seat. He closed the door and rounded the truck, getting into the driver side.

Aurelie smiled. "I like your cousin."

"He's a good man," Beau said. "You'd like their entire family. They can be a little overwhelming, especially when you have them all together at one time. But they don't know a stranger, and they make you feel like one of the family from day one. I always loved coming to visit."

Aurelie stared out the front windshield as they drove away. "You really are lucky to have a big family. It must be nice."

Beau shrugged. "Depends on the day of the week. It can be great, and it can be a pain in the ass. Sometimes, you just want to get away from them."

"At least you have a choice of being with them or getting away," she said. "When you're an only child, you don't have that choice."

He shot a glance toward her. "Was it lonely growing up without brothers and sisters?"

Aurelie lifted a shoulder and let it fall. "For the most part, as an only child, you don't know what you're missing. It was when I was with my friends who had siblings that I could see how it could be, good and bad. I always wished I had at least one brother or sister. As it was, my mom and my dad were my friends when my friends weren't around. It's not the same as having another kid to pay with. I was around adults more than I was around children, except in school."

"Well, you're welcome to borrow any of my siblings whenever you get a hankering for a brother or sister," Beau offered. "Just be aware that they might kick, pull your hair or spit."

Aurelie laughed. "Nice of you to offer them. They may not agree to being loaned out."

"They're all pretty outgoing. They like meeting new people and making friends." He smiled. "I'm sure they'd love you."

"Thanks." The corners of Aurelie's lips tipped upward in a thoughtful smile.

As he drove into Bayou Mambaloa, Beau made a decision and a detour to the old boat factory. "Remember when I said I have some friends who might be able to help us?"

She nodded.

"I'd like you to meet them," he said. "They could help determine who's targeting you."

"I'll take any help I can get," she said. "Are they in law enforcement?"

"Not exactly," Beau said. He didn't know how much to tell her, but he wanted to tap into the resources Brotherhood Protectors had available to them. The sooner they did, the better.

"My friends are former military men, like me, from various branches, all former special forces. They belong to an organization called the Brotherhood Protectors. They have special assets available to them that could help us search through the backgrounds of people you've come into contact with. They might also be able to keep up with the sheriff's department. They could tap into information about the case and feed that back to us in a timelier manner. That way, we won't have to stop at the sheriff's office several times a day."

"That sounds good. Anything they can do to help would be great." Her eyes narrowed. "So, they're protectors? Is that like bodyguards? Or are they more like private investigators?"

"A little bit of both. They're also capable of rescuing people in tight situations, like if somebody was kidnapped and held hostage. Those of us who were in Special Operations on active duty performed missions like that. We went in and extracted individuals who were held as prisoners or hostages for ransom."

Aurelie stared across the console at him. "Are they performing these functions in a civilian capacity now that they're out of the military?" Aurelie asked.

Beau nodded, bracing for when she realized his connection to the brotherhood and her.

Her frown deepened, and she tipped her head to the side. "Your cousin said something about your new job." She shot a narrow-eyed glance toward him. "Are you working for the Brotherhood Protectors with your friends?"

The woman wasn't stupid. Beau wouldn't pretend that she was, and he wouldn't continue to lie. "I am."

"Sounds interesting and exciting," she said. "Is there much call for that kind of service?"

"More than you think," Beau said.

"It's sad to think there's enough trouble at home that we need a service like that. But I guess I'm glad there are people like you and your friends who are qualified to handle it."

He glanced in her direction again, trying to read into her expression and body language.

She stared straight-faced at the boat factory as they approached.

He had no clue what she was thinking, which made Beau even more nervous than if she'd blasted him for not telling her that he was her bodyguard.

Whatever was going through her mind, he would weather it when it hit. Right now, he needed his team to work on finding out who had attacked her, who had trashed her home and was continuing to send death threats. If it pissed her off that her father had hired him to be her bodyguard, she'd have to get over it. The goal was to keep her safe. He needed all the help he could get.

He pulled into the parking lot at the old boat factory.

Aurelie frowned. "This is a boat factory. Why are we here?"

Beau parked and turned off the engine. "This is the Bayou Brotherhood Protectors' headquarters."

"Then why does that sign say Boat Factory on it?" she asked, her voice sharp, impatient.

He turned off the engine and stared at the building. "Because it's also a boat factory."

"Humph," she muttered.

Based on the tension in her tone, Beau had to believe she knew.

At least now, he could work openly with his teammates.

She could be mad and even hate him. He told himself that as long as he kept her safe and alive, it didn't matter.

But it did.

CHAPTER 9

AURELIE DIDN'T WAIT for Beau to come around and open her door for her. As soon as he parked in the parking lot at the boat factory, she pushed open the door and dropped down. Inside, she was steaming. She focused on keeping her face from showing what was going on in her head.

Beau worked for the Brotherhood Protectors.

She should've known. This had to be her father's work. Then she remembered. She could not remember telling her father the name of her protector. Yet, her father had known his name was Beau.

How incredibly stupid of her.

She wasn't sure who she was madder at, her father, Beau or herself. Her father for hiring a bodyguard without her permission or knowledge. Beau, for taking the job but not letting her know he was a bodyguard, conning her into falling for him. Plus,

ELLE JAMES

he'd used that lame excuse that when you saved a person, you were responsible for them for the rest of their life.

Bull-fucking-shit!

She was mad at herself for falling for all of it. And for falling for Beau. He was a hired bodyguard, not someone truly interested in her for herself.

She was the job.

She followed him to the door of the old boat factory without saying a word. If she didn't need the help as badly as she did, she would've told him to go fuck himself and then found a way back to Baton Rouge to get a car and go...

Where?

She could stay at her father's house. No. She'd moved out to start living her own life. Leaving her father had taken a huge emotional toll on her and her father. She didn't want to put him through it again. Nor herself. Her father needed to move on and find another partner to share his life with besides his only daughter. He deserved a second chance at love.

He'd said that Aurelie deserved the same. Only this time, she needed to find someone worthy of her love.

Aurelie had no intention of dating or looking for love. It was too hard. Too messy. Too painful when it didn't work out.

She could go back to her house and hope that

whoever had ransacked it wouldn't feel the need to do it again, only with her in it this time.

No. Not an option.

She couldn't go back to her house yet.

For the moment, she'd play her next move by ear. She'd see what the Brotherhood Protectors had to offer in the way of finding the one responsible for her troubles. Between the Brotherhood Protectors and the elements of law enforcement that were investigating the attacks, they should come up with something. As soon as they found the person responsible and put him in jail, Aurelie could walk away from Beau and never have to look at him again.

Beau opened the boat factory door and held it for her.

She stepped through, careful not to touch him and spark that electric shock that happened every time since she'd met him.

Expecting an old boat factory, she was surprised at how shiny and fresh everything was inside. New machines lined each side of the large building with aluminum stacked in neat piles or rolls, ready to be fed into the machines to make small boats.

"When our founder, Hank Patterson, was looking for a place to set up shop in the bayou, we found this old, abandoned boat factory. Hank decided to use it as the base of operations for the Bayou Brother Protectors. Our division leader, Remy Montagne, convinced him it would be a good idea to keep it as a boat factory as cover for the operations center for the Bayou Brotherhood Protectors—and it would give our team purpose between jobs if they could manufacture boats at the same time. Hank had the old factory outfitted with new equipment to manufacture small skiffs. He hired a full-time manager who was experienced in the manufacturing techniques needed to make boats. That man is responsible for training us and keeping operations flowing on a limited basis."

"You know how to run this machinery?" she asked, despite her desire not to talk to the man. Curiosity got the better ever.

"I do," Beau said. "Building something with your hands and operating machines is therapeutic. A lot of our guys coming off active duty need that."

"PTSD?" She shot a glance toward Beau. He'd been in a helicopter crash and lost members of his team. She was sure that, having been an Army Ranger, he'd seen battle and the horrors of war. That had to have been hard. Coming back to the civilian world where people didn't understand that life had to be even harder. Did he have PTSD?

Her anger lessened a little. But she wasn't ready to let go of it altogether. There was no excuse for him lying to her about why he was there at that masquerade ball in the first place. And the kiss? Had that all been part of the job?

Her anger spiked all over again. She wanted to ask him for the truth, but not here. Not now.

Beau led her through the boat factory to a door on the back wall. To enter this section, he had to put a finger on a fingerprint reader and then look into a retinal scanner. Once he passed both security checks, a lock disengaged. He pushed the door open to reveal a hallway. As soon as he stepped through, lights blinked on.

They walked past several closed doors to one at the end of the corridor. It opened into a large conference room with a huge table dominating the center, a giant screen on one wall and a bank of computers and monitors taking up another wall.

A man sat at the conference table with a laptop in front of him. When the door opened, he looked up and then pushed to his feet. He rounded the table and met Beau and Aurelie holding out his hand. "Beau," he said. "I'm glad you stopped by." He shook hands with Beau and then turned to Aurelie. "You must be Miss Anderson." He held out his hand toward her.

Her lips pressed into a tight line. "You know who I am, but I don't know you."

"My name is Remy Montagne. Beau told us you two were coming," the man said. "He asked us for help figuring out what's going on with his..." the man clamped his lips shut for a moment and then continued with, "with you."

"His assignment," Aurelie corrected.

Remy flashed a look at Beau. "Did you..."

Beau shook his head. "No."

Aurelie looked from one man to the other, her jaw hardening. "I'm right, aren't I? I'm Mr. Boyette's assignment...? He's my bodyguard...?"

Remy nodded. "Yes."

Aurelie couldn't look at Beau. "When did he get the assignment?"

Remy glanced at Beau.

Beau answered, "The morning of the masquerade ball."

"Your father called us that morning and asked us to provide protection for you since you were getting death threats." Remy tipped his head toward Beau. "Our guy, Beau, got the assignment. Your father asked that he not let you know that he was there to protect you. He was afraid that you would reject the idea. All he wanted to do was keep you safe."

Aurelie faced Beau. "Is that how it was?"

Beau nodded. "I was under strict orders not to let you know I was there to protect you."

Her lips pressed together as she breathed in and out through her nose before responding. "I see. Does my father know that you told me?"

Beau shook his head. "Not yet."

"Good," she said. "Let me do the honors."

Beau dipped his head.

Aurelie lifted her chin and turned to Remy. "What can you do to help me?"

"I'm sure you've already gone through this with the sheriff," Remy said. "It would really help if you could repeat the information so that we can get to work on it."

"What information do you need?" she asked.

"Information about anyone who might have an issue with you, your work or your father." Remy raised a finger for each item. "Names of old boyfriends, rejected lovers, the mailman, basically anyone you might have pissed off in the last few weeks or months."

"I've been too busy working for my father for lovers or boyfriends," she said. "You can mark them off your list."

"What about your work with your father? I understand your philanthropy effort is to save the bayou," Remy said. "Are you meeting resistance with the work you're doing?"

She nodded.

"If I could get a list of the corporations or individuals you've encountered recently, that would be a good place to start," Remy said. "We can run background checks on them. "

"It would help if I had my laptop," Aurelie said. "Unfortunately, it's in my car in Baton Rouge at my father's house."

Remy gave a hint of a smile. "I could have someone retrieve it for you."

"I'd appreciate it if you could have someone give me a ride up to Baton Rouge to get my car," she said.

"Beau will do that," Remy said.

"I'd rather have someone else." She lifted her chin. "Someone who hasn't lied to me."

BEAU HAD EXPECTED HER REACTION, but it still hurt. He hadn't wanted to keep the truth from her. Knowing her past with the boyfriend who'd turned out to be married, he understood her anger. He'd violated her trust. He wouldn't get that back anytime soon. He'd have to earn it by proving he would never intentionally hurt her.

If she gave him the opportunity to do so. The way it appeared, she was about to shut him out of her life altogether.

"Miss Anderson," Remy started.

"Aurelie," she corrected.

"Aurelie," he started again, "Beau got the assignment because the other members of the team were unavailable." He spread his arms wide. "I'd take you myself, but I can't today. If you can wait until tomorrow, I might find room on my schedule."

Her brow furrowed. "That's fine. I'll find my own ride."

"Miss Anderson—Aurelie," Remy said. "You're in mortal danger. No matter how you feel about Beau, he will keep you safe. Let him do his job. If you still feel the same tomorrow, I'll take you to Baton Rouge myself. But, please, let Beau provide the protection you need until then."

Her pretty lips pressed into a thin line. For a long moment, she didn't respond, as if going over her options in her mind.

Finally, she nodded. "Okay. Only until tomorrow. Get me to Baton Rouge, where I'll have a discussion with my father, and Brotherhood Protectors will be relieved of responsibility for my safety."

Remy dipped his head. "Agreed."

No! No! No!

Beau's instinctive reaction was to argue and shake some sense into Aurelie. He sensed she was too angry at that moment to listen. He might as well talk to a wall. The hard-headed woman needed time to cool off.

He'd apologize and promise to be completely transparent from that moment forward. It might not make a difference, but he had to try. She might be the client, but she was beginning to be more than just the job. Hell, she'd been more than just a client from when he'd pulled her into his arms on the dance floor.

Something about her drew him to her like no other woman had ever achieved.

She was strong, independent and knew what she wanted and didn't want. He couldn't let anything happen to her. If she fired him, he'd still follow her around to make sure she didn't end up in the bayou with the alligators again, or worse.

Remy met Beau's gaze. "Let me know what you need me to do in the morning."

Beau gave a brief nod. "Yes, sir."

Remy's gaze returned to Aurelie. "Beau will protect you. You don't have to like him but let him do his job. I'm sure you're perfectly capable of taking care of yourself, but you don't have eyes in the back of your head. Beau has your six. He'll make sure you're safe. The Brotherhood Protectors are trained to work as a team, to have each other's backs. It's how we survived on the battlefield."

Aurelie sighed. "I hear you."

"Now, if you'll excuse me," Remy said. "I want to feed your information to our computer guru in the main office. Swede is a master at finding information on the internet and the dark web."

Aurelie's eyebrows shot up. "Dark web?"

Remy nodded. "He checks all the information on all the databases he can access. If someone has a dark past, he'll find it."

She nodded again. "Good."

"I'll have him look into your father's opponent, too."

"Why would his opponent target me? If he didn't want competition, wouldn't he eliminate it? Why would he go after me?"

"We need to cover every angle," Remy said.

"Sometimes, the most bizarre ideas prove to be the ones that solve the case."

"We'll be at Old Man Pearson's house. Do you know where that is?" Beau asked.

Remy nodded. "We used to go swimming off his dock in the summertime."

Beau chuckled. "Elise mentioned that it was a favorite of her peers. I don't remember swimming there as a teen."

"Old Man Pearson never minded. It was in a cove that few boats entered. We didn't have to worry about being run over by fishing boats or party barges."

Beau shook his head. "I must have spent too many summers in Bayou Miste with my cousins. I'll have to give it a try."

"You should," Remy said with a smile. "Let me know if you need backup. I'll have my phone on me in case of emergencies."

"Will do." Beau glanced at Aurelie, who still wasn't meeting his gaze. His heart pinched hard in his chest. All he could do was to keep moving. Hopefully, Aurelie would come around. "Ready?"

She gave a quick nod, spun on her heels and marched for the door.

Beau cast a twisted smile at Remy.

"Give her a minute to process," Remy whispered. "She'll realize it wasn't your fault. Her father gave us strict instructions not to tell her."

"So, now we've broken his trust as well." Beau snorted. "Sometimes you win, sometimes you lose."

"And sometimes, you're rained out." Remy grinned and clapped a hand on Beau's back. "It all works out in the end. Give it time."

Give Aurelie time, Beau added silently.

She waited for him at the doorway that led into the boat factory.

He opened the door for her and waited while she passed through it. Her shoulder brushed against his, sending a spark across his nerves, pinging through his body like a ball in a pinball machine. When heat settled at his core, he pushed back against the rising tide of desire.

He had to get a firm grip. The woman wanted nothing to do with him.

Beau made another stop before heading for the safe house. He pulled into the parking lot at Broussard's Country Store.

When he went to get out of the truck, Aurelie sat still.

"Aren't you going inside? You need conditioner and other things to tide you over for a while."

She stared straight ahead. "I don't need anything."

He frowned. She damn well did need stuff. "It's not fancy, and they might not carry the brands you prefer, but it's better than nothing."

"I can get by for one more night."

He stared at her for a moment longer. "Why sacrifice when you don't have to?"

Her brow formed a V over her nose. She spun to face him, her cheeks bright pink. "Damn it, I don't have my purse. I don't have money, and I refuse to be a charity case to you."

Beau could have smacked his forehead. She had told him the night before that she'd left her purse in her father's car.

"I have money." He pulled his wallet out of his back pocket, dug bills and a credit card out of the pockets and tried to hand them to her.

She held up her hands. "No. I can't take your money."

"Then show me what you like, what will fit, and I'll buy them as gifts." He sighed. "At the very least, you need shampoo and conditioner, and we need food for dinner."

"I'm not hungry," she said with a stubborn tilt of her head.

"Well, I am," Beau said more forcefully than he'd intended. He drew in a breath and started over. "I'm sorry. Our last meal was breakfast, we missed lunch and I'm getting hangry. I'd like to buy some food to prepare at the cottage."

"Go on," she said, waving a hand. "Get your food. I'll wait here."

He shook his head. "I can't leave you in the truck.

I don't feel comfortable letting you out of my sight for a moment."

"No one is going to attack me so close to a public place," she said. "Besides, I'll be in the truck with the doors locked."

"Are you one hundred percent certain you'll be safe?" he challenged. "Are you willing to bet your life on it?"

She nodded.

He crossed his arms over his chest. "Have you heard of drive-by shootings?"

Her brow dipped. "Yes."

"That's all it takes. A car and a gun. The truck doors and windows aren't built to repel bullets."

She stared at the store for a moment, then sighed. "Fine. I'll go in with you."

"Thank you," he said softly and got out.

CHAPTER 10

AURELIE WALKED with Beau into the Broussard Country Store.

They hadn't gone three steps inside when a small child raced toward them, slammed into Beau's legs, giggled and shouted over his shoulder, "Can't catch me!"

"Yes, I can!" Another little boy rounded the end of a row of shelves containing an array of potato chips, nuts and candy.

"Alan, Jr!" A woman's voice called out. "Stop right there!"

The trailing boy skidded to a stop and turned around. "But Bodie hit me with a shoe."

"I don't care what he hit you with. You know the rules. No running in the store. Bodie. Here. Now."

The little boy who'd run into Beau slipped behind him.

Chrissy Broussard, the store owner's wife, appeared at the end of the aisles. When she spotted the adults standing in the doorway, her eyes widened. "Oh. Sorry. Alan had to run some groceries to Widow Willie. She's not feeling well enough to get out and do her own shopping. I'm managing the store and five hellions at once. Two of them escaped the back room where I have the one-eyed babysitter tuned into cartoons."

Beau frowned.

Chrissy sighed. "One-eyed babysitter? Never heard it called that?" She shook her head. "Television."

Beau chuckled. "You should call Gerard. I'm sure he'd come help."

"I did. He and Bernie are in the middle of harvesting their melon patches. They're short hands and couldn't spare a minute. Besides, Alan said he'd only be fifteen minutes." Chrissy checked the watch on her wrist. "And that was thirty minutes ago. I'm sure Willie is talking non-stop. She loves visitors and hasn't gotten many since her daughter and son-in-law moved to Houston." She looked up and forced a smile. "Who have you got with you?"

Beau turned. "Chrissy Broussard, this is Auri," he said, shortening her name at the last second in case anyone came asking if Aurelie Anderson had been seen in town. "She's a friend of mine."

Chrissy held out her hand with a smile. "Auri, what a pretty name. Welcome to our little store."

Aurelie shook Chrissy's hand. "Nice to meet you. You have a lovely store. It's very—"

"Cluttered, disorganized, a zoo with children running down the aisles?" Chrissy gave a harried laugh.

"I was going to say quaint and kind of retro." Aurelie looked around. "I like the old-fashioned feel."

Chrissy smiled at Beau. "I like your friend." She turned back to Aurelie. "I'm working on reorganizing products on the shelves, so it can be confusing trying to find things. Tell me what you want, and I'll help you locate it."

Aurelie glanced at Beau first, then faced Chrissy. "I could use some shampoo and conditioner."

"Perfect. I just started stocking some of the name brands that are so popular." She turned to the boy at her side. "Alan, Jr., take Bodie to the back room. You can all have a cookie if you're nice. Just one. I don't want you bouncing off the walls before bedtime." She looped Aurelie's hand around her elbow. "Come with me. I'll get you fixed up."

Bodie left his safe space behind Beau's legs and hurried to follow his brother to the back of the store, where they'd enjoy a cookie before bed.

Beau's gaze followed the two women as they headed for the health and beauty aisle. Keeping an eye on the door, he grabbed a cart and headed for the food and produce section, where he selected shrimp, chicken, smoked sausage, rice, a small package of flour, chicken broth, butter, salt, pepper and Cajun seasoning. In the produce department, he chose an onion, celery and carrots. All the ingredients he needed for gumbo the way his mother made it. He might not know how to cook many things, but gumbo was something he'd mastered as a teen. He picked up bananas, apples, grapes, crackers and cheese for snacks, a carton of eggs and a pound of bacon for breakfast. He added orange juice, coffee, creamer, a bottle of red wine and a loaf of bread to the cart and rolled it to the checkout counter.

Chrissy and Aurelie soon joined him with their arms full of shampoo, conditioner, a brush, curling iron, moisturizer and an assortment of makeup.

As Aurelie passed him, she murmured quietly, "I'll pay you back." She glanced at his cart and blinked. "Are you planning to feed an army?"

"Maybe." Beau shrugged.

Chrissy chuckled. "Hungry?"

"It's never good to shop for food when you're hungry."

"Tell me about it. We still have to cook all this."

"Then I better check you out so you can get going." Chrissy quickly rang up their purchases.

Beau paid with his credit card, and the three of them fit all the groceries into plastic bags.

When they were done, Chrissy smiled. "I hope to see you again soon, Auri. You'll like Bayou Mambaloa. We're lucky that the Brotherhood Protectors chose our little town as their southern headquarters. They're a great group of men. Remy saved my sister's life. I can't sing their praises loud enough."

"Thank you for all your help and making me feel welcome," Aurelie said.

They carried the bags of groceries out and stowed them in the back seat of the pickup.

Beau drove the short distance to the other side of town, turned off Main Street and onto the road leading to the secluded house on the bayou.

He found the location incredibly beautiful in its solitude. No houses were nearby, no noisy roads with trucks rumbling or motorcycles roaring past all day and night. If he liked it enough, he might consider purchasing the house and land. Yeah, it needed a lot of work to bring it up to date, but he was handy with tools, and there was always an online video with instructions on just about everything.

It would be everything he'd dreamed of owning, but it needed more than just handiwork to make it a home.

It needed a woman. Immediately, Aurelie came to mind. He could picture her sitting beside him in one of the rocking chairs on the porch with half a dozen children playing at their feet. Some of them would have her dark hair and brown eyes. The rest would be blond with his blue eyes.

What was he thinking? You didn't start thinking of marriage and children with a woman you'd only met the night before. It took time to get to know each other and fall in love, didn't it?

As he parked in front of the house, Beau's breath lodged in his throat. He stared at the house, the images in his mind running rampant.

This was crazy. Hunger was making him hallucinate. There was no other reason for him to dream of being married to Aurelie and spawning so many children.

She was a senator's daughter used to country clubs and formal events. She'd never go for a guy who would be happiest living in a backwater town on the bayou.

Focus.

Beau pulled his gun out of the console, shoved open his door and leaped out as if his seat were on fire. After shoving the pistol into his waistband, he slung her gym bag over his shoulder, grabbed most of the grocery bags and hurried up the steps of the porch.

"You must be starving." Aurelie followed a few steps behind, carrying the rest of the bags.

"I am," he said. "And we still have to cook the food."

"I'm still mad at you," she said, "but I'll help."

"So noted." Beau inserted the key into the lock and opened the door. He stepped across the threshold and turned to her. "Stand just inside the door while I check for intruders."

She entered, closed the door behind her and waited while he made a quick pass through the cottage.

Beau dropped his bags by the door, pulled the gun from his waistband and then checked all the rooms and closets before he returned to her. "All clear."

Aurelie still held bags of groceries in her hands as she stared at him, her jaw tight, her chin raised. "I'm still not convinced this is a good idea."

"What? The part about making dinner or the part about staying here?"

"The part about staying here *with you*," she said.

He tucked the gun in his belt and gathered his bags. "I'm sorry. I can't undo what's been done, but I'll do my best to make it up to you by cooking the best gumbo in the bayou." He carried the bags into the kitchen and laid them on the counter.

"Gumbo doesn't erase the lies," she said as she followed him.

"I know." Beau couldn't win this argument and had no intention of trying. She'd been hurt by the lies of a married man. He stopped emptying the bags, crossed to where she stood and took her hands in his.

When she started to pull away, he held on a little tighter, but not so tight that she couldn't free herself if she really wanted to.

"I know that trust is hard won and never given lightly," he said. "I've violated your trust. You have every right to be angry with me. I wish you weren't mad, but I take full responsibility for my actions."

"As you should," she whispered.

He stared down into her eyes. "You have no reason to believe me, but I want you to know that if you choose to have someone else protect you, I'll understand. And though each one of my teammates is qualified to keep you safe, I would continue to shadow you until the bastard who nearly killed you last night is captured and put behind bars." He squeezed her hands gently, then let them go. "Now, let me cook that gumbo. You might feel better with a full belly."

"Food won't fix everything," she warned.

"Obviously, you haven't had my gumbo." Beau gave her a playful wink and finished unloading the bags.

Aurelie dug through the cabinets and found a cutting board, stock pot, saucepan, ladles and knives.

Beau washed out the sink and filled it with warm water and some dish soap he found in the cabinet below the sink. He made quick work of washing everything thoroughly before placing the stockpot and the saucepan on the stove.

BEAU

After cleaning the chicken, he placed it in the stockpot, filled it with water and fired up the burner. Next, he added a heavy dose of Cajun seasoning and pepper.

Aurelie came behind him and added more Cajun seasoning.

He chuckled. "So, you like it spicy?"

She nodded.

He patted his chest. "A woman after my own heart."

While the chicken cooked, he worked alongside Aurelie, chopping celery, onions and carrots and added them to the stockpot with the chicken.

Beau liked working alongside the senator's daughter in a comfortable silence. At least on his part. For all he knew, she could have been quietly dreaming up ways to make him suffer for lying to her. He chose to think otherwise and enjoyed the simple tasks of preparing food together. He could get used to bumping into her in the kitchen.

While in the Army, he'd given up on the idea of marriage, settling down roots and raising a family.

Now that he was back in Bayou Mambaloa, he remembered how good it felt to have a home and family.

In a saucepan, he dropped a stick of butter, let it melt and then added flour, stirring constantly until it formed a thick brown roux.

When the chicken was practically falling off the

bone, Beau fished it out of the stockpot, deboned and pulled it apart. He added the meat back to the stockpot along with the shrimp and sausage. He stirred in the roux and let it simmer while he cleaned the saucepan, filled it with water and set it on the stove to boil for the rice.

Aurelie stood over the stockpot, inhaling the flavorful steam rising from the gumbo. "It smells amazing."

"Tastes even better," Beau said. "It'll be another twenty minutes before the rice is done."

"I'm going to get a shower and put on some of my own clothes," Aurelie said. "Unless you need help with anything else."

Beau shook his head. "I've got it under control. It'll be ready when you are."

After Aurelie left the kitchen, Beau explored all the cabinets, making note of what needed to be cleaned, tossed and donated. If they weren't on the road to Baton Rouge the next day, they could start in the kitchen, sorting through Pearson's belongings.

It seemed sad to be sorting through a stranger's things, making decisions about whether to toss, donate or save items. Beau hoped that his family had loved him while he was alive and visited him often. Most of the items in the kitchen were old, yellowed or chipped. The pots and pans had loose or missing handles.

He wandered into the tiny dining room, which

had an old mahogany dining table and matching chairs that needed the seats recovered. The wood had stood the test of time. The chairs could be recovered, and the set would work for someone for another forty or fifty years.

In a cabinet against the wall, he found a nice set of porcelain dishes with a delicate rose pattern. He took two bowls from the set, found a couple of wine glasses and two settings of silverware, and carried them to the kitchen, where he washed and dried them.

With a rag he found in one of the kitchen drawers, he washed the dining table and placed the silverware and wine glasses on one end.

Back in the kitchen, he poured rice into boiling water and then searched through all the drawers until he located a corkscrew. He pulled the cork on the wine bottle and set it on the table along with a small plate of crackers and cheese and two candles he'd found in a drawer of the china cabinet.

By the time Aurelie returned to the kitchen, the rice was done, the table was set and wine had been poured.

"I thought we'd serve up the gumbo at the stove and carry it into the dining room," he said.

Aurelie scooped rice into her bowl and used the ladle to pour the gumbo on top.

Beau did the same.

They carried their bowls into the dining room and laid them on the table.

He held a chair for her and then sat in the one next to hers.

With a dramatic wave of his hand, Beau lifted his spoon. "*Bon appetit.*"

Aurelie dug into the gumbo, blew on the spoonful to cool it, then took a bite. She closed her eyes as she chewed, softly moaning. After she swallowed, she looked across the table at him. "Wow. That's amazing."

He grinned. "I'm glad you liked it. I'm hoping to bribe myself back into your good graces."

"It'll take a lot more than gumbo to get there," she said. "But this is a good start."

"That's all I can ask." He took a bite of the gumbo. As he chewed, he stole glances her way, loving how she got totally into eating the meal down to the very last bite, taking sips of wine along the way.

When they were done, they carried their dishes into the kitchen and worked together to rinse and stack them in the dishwasher.

Aurelie found a plastic storage container in a cabinet large enough to hold the rest of the gumbo.

They washed and dried the container and its lid, poured in the rice and gumbo and stored it in the refrigerator.

After they'd finished in the kitchen, Beau went around the house, checking door and window locks.

When he was satisfied that the locks would hold, he ducked into the single bathroom for a shower.

Aurelie had spent time scrubbing the tub, removing the shadow of a ring and making the old porcelain tub shine.

He rinsed the tub, dried off and wrapped the towel around his hips. Unlike Aurelie, Beau hadn't thought ahead to bring in his backpack that he kept stuffed behind the backseat in his truck, ready to go at a moment's notice.

With all intentions of wearing the same clothes he'd had on before the shower, he picked up his jeans from the floor, only to discover they were soaked. Apparently, he hadn't closed the shower curtain securely. Now, there was a puddle on the floor. His jeans had been lying in the middle of it.

His truck was only a few short steps away from the cottage. Rather than dress in sodden jeans, he could march his dumb ass out to his truck, grab his backpack and return in less than a minute. If he was lucky, he wouldn't run into Aurelie on the way out or the way back.

Beau stepped out of the bathroom and almost ran into Aurelie where she stood precariously on a rickety chair, unscrewing the globe on a ceiling light fixture.

When she looked his way, she lost her balance and the chair teetered.

Beau darted forward and caught her before she

hit the floor. In the process, he released the grip on his towel, and it dropped to the floor. He held her in his arms, crushing her to his chest, his pulse racing. "Are you all right?"

She nodded. "I was trying to change the lightbulb."

Beau blew out a shaky breath. "Geez, woman. Let me help you with those. I'm a little taller."

"I could've done it myself," she said.

"I know," he said. "But if you have somebody nearby, it's always good if they have your back."

"True." Aurelie grimaced. "Even better if you use a proper stepladder, instead of an old chair." She glanced down at the remains of the wooden chair that lay in splinters on the floor.

"Don't worry about it," he said. "I'll clean that up."

"It's okay. I'll do it," Aurelie said. "As soon as you put me down."

Beau shook his head. "Not a good idea," he said. "Not unless you want to get an eyeful."

Her brow furrowed. "What do you mean?"

Beau's lips twisted into a broad grin. "It was either catch you or save my dignity." He gave a pointed look at the towel lying on the floor.

Aurelie's eyes widened, and her mouth formed an O. "I see," she said. "What if I close my eyes?"

He grinned. "That's totally up to you."

Her cheeks reddened. "I'm closing my eyes." And she did.

Beau lowered her legs, and let her body slide down his naked one. His arms remained around her, holding her close until she was steady on her feet.

Aurelie rested her hands on his bare chest and opened her eyes. Making no move to step away, she looked up into his eyes, her lips parting ever so softly.

Electricity zinged through his body from every point where she touched him, making his pulse race and blood heat.

"I just want to know one thing," she said.

"Yes," he croaked, barely able to push air past his strangled vocal cords.

Her tongue swept across rosy lips.

At that moment, he wanted to kiss her so badly it was almost a physical pain to resist.

"That kiss…" she whispered, "was it all part of the lie?"

Beau's control snapped. He bent and claimed those lips in a hard, desperate kiss. One hand clamped on the small of her back, pressing her close while the other cupped the back of her head, bringing her in impossibly closer. He plundered her mouth, pushing his tongue past her teeth to caress hers in long, languorous strokes.

The hands on his chest slid upward, lacing behind his neck. Her body leaned into his.

Time stood still as Beau lost himself in her arms.

When breathing became a necessity, he reluctantly raised his head and stared down at her flushed cheeks and swollen lips. "It wasn't a lie," he said his voice gruff.

"That wasn't just a kiss?"

Beau groaned. "No."

"I know my father hired you," she said. "You don't have to pretend to keep me in line."

Beau laughed. "Does this feel like I'm pretending?" He pulled her hips against his, his engorged cock nudging her soft belly. "Woman, you do crazy things to me. You make me lose control. And, sweetheart, that can be dangerous."

Her eyes widened, and her breathing became more ragged. Slowly, she shook her head. "But a man can feel lust without making a deep connection."

"True," he said, "but I've never lost control with a woman before. Now, either you step away, or I'm going to lose my mind."

She stared up into his eyes. "I found clean sheets in the closet. I used them to make the bed in the master bedroom." She left the words hanging between them. When he didn't move, she added, "I'm not stepping away."

Beau sucked in a shaky breath. "Are you sure?"

She nodded. "Even if it doesn't mean anything. I understand. I just don't want you to do it because you think it's part of the job. And yes, we barely know each other, but I don't care. I'll worry about that tomorrow."

That was the problem. Beau barely knew this woman, yet he didn't want to let her out of his arms for even a second. The right thing to do would be to set her on her feet and walk away. Instead, his arms tightened around her, and he turned, strode into the master bedroom and kicked the door closed behind them.

CHAPTER 11

WHAT WAS SHE DOING? Was she insane?

Aurelie opened mouth to tell Beau that she'd changed her mind. That she'd made a mistake.

Her lips parted but all that came out was a moan.

Beau laid her on the clean sheets and dropped on the bed beside her. He leaned up on his elbow and stared down into her eyes. He brushed a strand of her hair back from her forehead and then cupped her cheek in his palm. "Now, is the time for you to change your mind." He shook his head and gave her a gentle smile. "Tell me to get lost, and I'll leave this room. Otherwise, I'm going to explore every inch of your beautiful body and then make mad, passionate love to you." He spoke the words and barely more than a whisper.

Her body reacted instantly, flushing with a heat so profound, she feared she'd spontaneously combust.

All thoughts of changing her mind flew out the window. She wanted him more than she'd ever wanted a man in her life. Her affair with the married man paled in comparison.

With her thoughts whirling, she couldn't form the right words. Knowing actions spoke louder, she raised shaking hands to the hem of her shirt and dragged it up her body.

Beau helped her divest herself of the blouse, tossing it over his shoulder. It hit the wall and slid to the floor.

Reaching beneath her, he unhooked her bra and slid the straps off her arms, freeing her breasts. Beau bent to kiss her below her ear, searing a path down to the pulse beating at the base of her neck. His mouth moved lower to capture a nipple between his lips.

Aurelie sucked air into her lungs, her back arching off the mattress, sensations burning across her nerves, coiling low in her belly.

Beau moved to the other breast, cupped it in his palm and teased the nipple with his teeth and tongue until it formed a tight little nub.

Her breathing grew labored, her body on fire. Aurelie writhed beneath Beau as he worked his way down her body, kissing a rib, tonguing her inner elbow, nipping at the skin just above the waistband of her pants.

He worked loose the top button and pushed the

jeans and her panties down her legs and off, leaving them where they fell.

Aurelie lay naked against the sheets, the light on the nightstand casting an intimate glow around them.

Beau leaned up on his arms. His gaze swept over her body and his eyes flared. "You're so damned beautiful."

Having a man who wasn't much more than a stranger staring down at her should have made her self-conscious, maybe a little embarrassed.

She wasn't.

The heat of his gaze couldn't be faked, nor could the length and thickness of his cock. Even if all he felt for her was lust, it was real and... intoxicating.

Aurelie reached out to capture his face between her palms. She leaned up and pressed her lips to his.

He came down on her, crushing her mouth with his in a kiss that rocked her world.

"I want you," Aurelie said against his lips. "Now. Inside me. Please."

When he came back up for air, he drew in a deep breath and let it out slowly. He pressed a finger to her lips. "Hold that thought."

"Huh?"

He leaped off the bed and left the bedroom.

She sat up, the heat of the moment fading without his body there to fan the flames. "Beau?"

Had she scared him away by telling him she wanted him?

Aurelie swung her legs over the side of the bed.

Before she could rise to her feet, he was back.

He frowned when he saw her sitting up. "Where are you going?"

"To find you," she answered. "Did I say something wrong?"

Beau chuckled. "No. In fact, you said all the right things. I just wasn't ready. As beautiful as our babies would be, I don't think we're ready for that kind of commitment." He held up a small packet and grinned. "Protection."

The weight lifted off Aurelie's chest and she laughed. "Of course." She smiled, glad he'd had the foresight to think of protection when all she could think about was getting it on. "Now, where were we?"

Beau advanced into the room and stopped in front of her. He cupped the back of her neck and bent down until his lips hovered over hers. "I don't remember exactly where we were, but this is a good place to start."

Then he kissed her, easing her backward until she lay on the mattress, her legs still dangling over the side.

He stroked her tongue with his and then moved lower, kissing his way down the length of her neck, across her collar bone to capture a nipple between his teeth. For several seconds he teased the nipple with his tongue and his teeth, then moved lower, kissing and flicking his tongue across her belly.

When Aurelie parted her legs, he dropped to his knees between her thighs and splayed his big hand over her sex.

Her heart pounded against her ribs, her breathing growing more erratic with every brush of his lips or touch of his hands.

Beau parted her folds and dragged a finger across her clit.

Aurelie sucked in a breath and held it, willing him to do that again.

That finger moved lower, pausing at her entrance for a moment before dipping into the slick channel.

She tipped her head back, expelling the pent-up breath only to suck another quick breath in and hold it.

As Beau's finger swirled inside her, he touched his tongue to her clit, flicking it gently once...twice.

Then, matching the rhythm of his finger inside her, he swirled his tongue around and around that nubbin of flesh and highly excited nerves, stroking, teasing and coaxing her up to the very edge of the earth. Teetering on the edge, all it took was one more flick of his tongue and she exploded in a kaleido-scope of sensations that rippled like a million bolts of lightning ricocheting throughout her body.

Aurelie clutched his head between her hands, her

finger digging into his hair, holding him there, milking her orgasm to the very last shiver of her release.

When she fell back to earth, she collapsed against the sheets, spent, yet still...incomplete.

After several deep breaths, she tugged on his hair. "Please," she begged. "I want you. Inside me."

He rose up over her, lifted her legs onto the bed and climbed in beside her.

His lips met hers, tasting of her sex. Then he reached for the condom, tore it open with his teeth and pulled it from the package.

When he leaned up on one hand to apply the protection, Aurelie took it from his hand.

"Let me," she said and gently pushed him over until he lay on his back, his cock hard, straight and ready for her.

Knowing she'd brought him to that state, gave her a feeling of power. Sitting up beside him, she fondled his balls and then wrapped her hand around his length, smoothing her fingers up and down the velvety soft skin, encasing his hard shaft.

She pumped her hand up and down several times until Beau caught her wrist in. "I won't last much longer if you keep doing that." He released her wrist.

Her lips curled on the corners as she slid her fingers down his cock and cupped his balls, rolling them between her fingers.

Beau groaned.

Aurelie chuckled and applied the condom, rolling it down over his cock. Then she straddled him and lowered herself over him. The few men she'd had sex with always wanted to be on top. She liked being in control.

Once Beau positioned his shaft at her entrance, Aurelie sank lower, taking him inside her channel, easing onto his length and girth. When she was fully seated, she leaned forward and pressed her lips to his in a brief kiss. Slowly, she moved up and down, loving the feeling of him inside her, filling her completely.

Beau's hands gripped her ass, increasing the speed. After a minute or two of her rocking his cock, his fingers dug into her flesh, and he lifted her off of him.

"Hey," she said. "I wasn't finished."

He flipped her onto her back and leaned over her. "Good, neither am I."

Beau slipped between her legs and touched the tip of his cock to her sex. "I need to move. To thrust deep inside you. Hard. Fast. Now." He draped her knees over his arms, gripped her thighs and drove into her just as he'd said...hard and fast. He pulled almost all the way out, then thrust again and again, moving faster each time until he rocked the bedframe, making it bang against the wall.

Her fingers dug into his tight ass, urging him to keep going, the tension rising like a tide within until it threatened to lift her and toss her to the heavens. Just when she thought it could not be any more intense, she exploded in an orgasm that shook her to her very core.

Aurelie gripped Beau's arms and held on as he thrust one last time, going deep, remaining buried inside her, his cock pulsing his release.

As she sank into the sheets, Beau lowered himself on top of her, his naked body warm against her heated flesh.

She didn't care that his weight made it difficult for her to catch her breath. She doubted she could draw air into her lungs even without him pressing against her. Their lovemaking had stolen her breath away. She could die in that moment convinced she'd had the best sex ever. There would be nothing to match it.

Unless, of course, they did it again. Her slowing pulse quickened.

Beau rolled to the side and took her with him, pulling her into his arm.

Aurelie rested her cheek against his chest, listening to the rapid beat of his heart, happy to know he was as stirred up as she was.

Beau's hand smoothed up and down her arm in slow sensuous strokes.

She twirled her finger around his small brown nipple. "Just so you know, I still don't trust you," she whispered.

His fingers stilled for only a second before he continued stroking her skin. "Even after the best... you've ever had?"

She gave his nipple a slight pinch. "How do you know that was the best sex I've ever had?"

"Did I say sex?" He raised an eyebrow. "Surely, you know I meant gumbo. Although, I have to admit the sex came in a close second."

"Are you kidding me?" Aurelie pushed up on her elbow, frowning. "Second?"

Beau chuckled and pulled her on top of him to kiss her soundly. "Okay, so maybe they tied for first," he whispered against her lips. "The main thing you need to know, is that I would never intentionally hurt you. I kind of like you and your sassy spirit."

She laid her head on his chest. "You're just saying that because you don't want me to fire you."

"You can't fire me," he said. "You didn't hire me."

"Isn't making love with me going against some rule or code of ethics?" she asked.

"Maybe if I worked for you."

"But you work for my father," she finished. "I'm still mad at you," she said. "I don't really know if I can trust you to tell me the truth."

"I'm not married," he said. "You can have our

computer guru give you all the data on me if you want proof."

"I just might," she said. "Swede, right?"

He nodded, his chin brushing against the crown of her head. "And Hank Patterson can vouch for me."

"Do you think they'll find me here?" she asked.

"I hope not." His arms wrapped around her, holding her close. "If they do, I'll keep you safe."

"I'm counting on it."

A muffled thump sounded from somewhere else in the house.

Aurelie froze. "Did you hear that?" she whispered.

Beau rolled her off him. He slipped out of the bed, pulled on his jeans and reached for the handgun he'd left on the dresser when he'd stripped for his shower.

Another muffled thump sounded through the closed door.

Aurelie leaped to her feet, grabbed her shirt from the floor and pulled it over her head. She found her pants where Beau had dropped them on the floor and dragged them up her legs, buttoning them at the waist.

"Stay here," he whispered.

The hell she would. If someone was out there, Beau was in as much danger as she was. Aurelie looked around the room for a weapon. All she could find was a pillow. She grabbed one from the bed and held it against her chest as Beau opened the door.

Something crashed in the kitchen.

Beau tiptoed down the hallway, the gun held in front of him.

Ignoring his order to stay, Aurelie followed with her pillow.

As they neared the kitchen door, a rustling sound was followed by scratching.

With only the starlight shining through the window of an open bedroom door to guide him, Beau held the gun in one hand and reached for the kitchen light switch.

Aurelie inched up behind him as he flipped the switch.

Light flooded the kitchen. A high-pitched yelp sounded.

Beau rounded the corner, Aurelie behind him.

He pointed the gun at the overturned trash and something hiding in the corner behind it. Too small to be a human, the creature hid behind the trash container a pale, brownish blob, visibly shaking.

Beau aimed the gun at the animal. "Stay back, it might be rabid."

The blob moved, darted out of its hiding place and ran straight for Beau and Aurelie.

As Beau aimed, Aurelie reached out and brought his hand down. "Don't."

She dropped to her haunches. When she did, the creature launched itself at her.

"Watch out!" Beau called out.

Aurelie opened her arms as the small animal leaped at her.

She fell backward, the animal landing on her chest.

"Aurelie!"

She struggled for a moment to grip the animal in her hands, her body shaking as she set the wiggling, mass of matted hair at arm's length. "What have we got here?" she said, staring through an impossible tangle of dirty brown fur at a black, button nose and a hint of black eyes buried in overgrown fur. "Are you a dog?" she asked, her eyes clouding with tears. "You poor baby. You can't even see through all that hair." She pulled the creature close as it snuggled against her, shivering in the heat.

Beau lowered his gun and sat on the floor beside Aurelie. "Are you sure it's a dog?"

"I think so," she said. "But it's so matted, it's hard to tell. Do you think it belonged to Old Man Pearson?"

"I can ask my mother in the morning. In the meantime, it's a biohazard. I'm sure it's covered in fleas and ticks and who knows what else."

"We have to do something for it. I can feel it's ribs through the matting. All the hair makes it look bigger than it is. I bet it doesn't weigh more than seven or eight pounds. I wonder how long it's been running wild." She pushed to her feet, the animal in her arms.

"If it was Pearson's dog, surely he had some way

of trimming its fur. I can't imagine he'd let it get this out of control while he was alive." Beau searched the cabinets, drawers and pantry for a set of clippers. He entered the laundry room and went through all the cabinets, finally finding an old pair of electric clippers.

"Thank God," Aurelie said.

"We should do this out on the porch." He carried the clippers outside, found an electric socket and plugged in the clippers.

Aurelie let go of the breath she'd held, praying the clippers would work. She held the pup while Beau sheared the matted hair off its body, a little at a time, careful not to nick its skin. When he was done, Aurelie looked down at a tiny, naked dog with big black eyes and a black nose.

"It's a female," Beau said. "She'll need a bath next. You'll need to drown the fleas and pluck the ticks."

Aurelie carried the dog to the kitchen where she filled the sink with warm water and placed the animal in it. Using dish soap, she scrubbed what was left of its fur, making the water cloudy with the dirt and grime she'd collected while running wild.

When she was sure the fleas were dead, Aurelie emptied the sink and rinsed the dog's fur once more.

Beau found a bowl, poured some of the dog food they'd found in the pantry into it and set it on the floor. He handed a towel to Aurelie.

After drying the animal, Aurelie set her on the

floor and watched as the little, now white, dog wolfed down the food Beau had given her.

Aurelie's heart squeezed hard in her chest. "She was starving. Look at those ribs."

"I never would have believed she was white." Beau shook his head. "What do you think she is?"

"Now that she's not matted, her hair is soft. I'd say she's maybe a mix between a poodle and maybe a Maltese?"

Beau found another bowl, filled it with water and set it beside the food bowl the dog was still working on. When he straightened he glanced at Aurelie. "What now?"

"I'll stay with her through the night," Aurelie said. "She's got to be frightened."

Beau sighed. "We'll do it together." He gathered blankets and made a pallet on the floor in the living room.

Aurelie monitored the dog while she ate, checking around the kitchen and laundry room. She discovered a small doggy door that had been cut out of the laundry room door leading out onto the back porch. She must have gotten in that way.

She placed an old laundry basket in front of the doggy door to keep the animal from exiting the way she'd gotten in. Now that people had returned to its home, she would be taken care of. The family might want to adopt it if it had belonged to Mr. Pearson.

Once the dog had eaten all the food in the bowl, it

drank for a long time and then collapsed on the cool tile floor.

Aurelie gathered it in her arms and carried it into the living room where Beau had made a pallet for them on the floor with blankets and pillows. She gave him a grateful smile and stretched out across the blanket.

"She's probably still got fleas," Beau said, dropping down beside Aurelie.

"I don't care. She's been lost for long enough." Aurelie tucked the dog close to her body, curling her arm around her. "I wonder what her name is?"

"I wouldn't get too attached," Beau warned. "If she was Pearson's dog, the family will want to take responsibility for it."

Aurelie frowned. "Then why didn't they do it sooner?" She curled her body around the animal and lay her head on the pillow. "What if they just abandoned her?" She smoothed her hand across the dog's back. "It's okay. You'll never be hungry again, my little cutie pie," she whispered into the dog's ear.

"Cutie pie, dog, it." She stared across at Beau. "She needs a name."

"Dog isn't good enough?" he said, his lips twitching.

Aurelie frowned. "She was someone's pet. She has a name, but what is it?" She stared at the pooch. "Maybe she'll respond to a name if we try a few?"

"How about Fifi?"

The dog didn't move or flick an ear.

"Marley," Aurelie said.

Nothing.

"Teddy," Beau tried. "Fred."

Aurelie's lips pressed together. "She's a girl."

"What?" Beau held up his hands. "A buddy of mine named his female retriever Fred."

Aurelie focused on the dog contentedly curled against her, eyes closed, breathing deeply. "Are you named after a flower? Rose, Daisy or Lily?"

The dog didn't lift her head or open an eye.

"Now that she's clean, she's white. What's white that would make a cute dog name?"

"Clouds, the moon, cotton?" Beau said. "Whitey?"

"Okay maybe they named her after someone famous like Betsy Ross or Harriet Tubman." She looked for any sign from the sleeping animal. "No?"

"How about someone in the movies? Pearson was old so maybe older movies?" Beau suggested.

"Betty Davis, Sophia Loren, Debbie Reynolds." The little dog didn't budge.

Beau's lips twisted. "How about a singer?"

"Doris Day, Rosemary Clooney, Olivia Newton John." Aurelie sighed. "She's not responding to anything."

"Don't give up now," Beau urged. "How about Pink, Cher, Adele or Lady Gaga?"

The dog's eyes opened, and she lifted her head to stare at Beau.

Aurelie touched Beau's arm. "One of those names got her attention. Say them again, only do it slowly."

"Pink." Beau said.

The dog tipped its head to the right.

"Cher," he said.

She tipped back to the left.

"Adele," Beau said.

No response.

Beau tried the last name. "Lady."

The little dog let out a sharp bark and wagged her tail.

Aurelie smiled. "Is that it? Is your name Lady?"

As if she'd been rescued all over again, she licked Aurelie's face, her tail wagging so hard her entire body moved with it.

Aurelie laughed and hugged her to her. "Lady, it is."

Beau shook his head and smiled at Aurelie. "The family isn't getting that dog back, are they?"

Aurelie pulled Lady closer. "Over my dead body."

"So, now I'm a bodyguard to a woman and a dog?" Beau shook his head. "I didn't sign up for this." He sighed. "Come here."

Aurelie didn't move from where she spooned her body around the bedraggled pup.

Beau got up, moved the blankets and pillows and settled behind Aurelie, spooning her body with his. "If you can't beat 'em, join 'em," he said as he rested his hand on Aurelie's hip.

She smiled, warm and secure in his arms. She still didn't trust him, but he had helped her rescue Lady. A man who stuck up for the underdog couldn't be all bad.

Maybe, just maybe, she'd give him a second chance.

CHAPTER 12

BEAU WOKE THE NEXT MORNING, his arm numb and his hip sore from lying on his side on the hardwood floor. Aurelie snuggled up against him, the pup curled in the crook of her arm.

As sore as he was from sleeping on a hard surface, he wouldn't change a thing.

This woman had captured his interest and possibly his heart from the moment he'd met her. Making love with her had been magical and something he wanted to do again and again. He could be perfectly content to make love with her every night and wake with her snuggled up against him every morning for the rest of his life.

But maybe on a mattress instead of the floor.

He had it good.

Too good?

How had he been lucky enough to come home

when the members of his Ranger squad hadn't been so fortunate?

Beau's euphoria threatened to fade as he remembered the faces of his fallen battle buddies. His mental therapist had encouraged him to look for the reasons he had been miraculously spared. The entire time he'd worked as a mercenary, guarding general contractors in Afghanistan, he hadn't seen any reason why he should have lived while his friends and brothers had died in the crash.

The memory of a man dressed all in black, throwing a woman over the boardwalk railing into the alligator-infested bayou, had made a believer out of Beau. If he hadn't been there, Aurelie might have drowned. If she had managed to fight her way to the surface, that alligator could have gotten to her before she'd found her way out of the water.

He'd been spared to save her.

And Aurelie had been spared her bayou death to save Lady, the abandoned stray.

In effect, Beau had been spared in the fiery crash so that he would be there to save Aurelie, who, in turn, saved Lady.

The gray light of dawn crept through the living room window, growing brighter with each passing minute.

Lady stirred in Aurelie's arm, waking the woman who'd saved her.

Beau remained on the floor, though his hip hurt

and he couldn't feel his arm. He wanted the quiet of the morning to last just a little longer.

It lasted another five seconds until Lady crawled over Aurelie's arm to lick Beau's face.

He grabbed the mutt and eased his arm from under Aurelie, trying not to wake her.

Lady danced on his chest, licking his chin, his cheek and his ears before Beau finally gave up, scooped the dog into his arms and rose from the floor. She probably needed to go outside.

As he tiptoed past Aurelie's inert form, her groggy voice murmured, "Put a leash on her. She might get scared and make a run for it."

With the dog tucked under his arm, Beau returned to the laundry room, where he'd found the clippers and located a small harness and a leash.

Lady turned circles in anticipation of going for a walk, making it difficult for Beau to get her into the harness and snap the lead onto it.

Once they were ready, Beau unlocked the laundry room door and walked out into the morning mist with what amounted to a dog that looked more like a rat and could possibly fit into a woman's purse.

Free of her heavily matted hair, Lady pranced out onto the porch and down the steps. Once out in the grass, she did her business, barked at the birds and trotted back to the porch, more than ready to return to the relative safety of the house.

Beau climbed the steps to find Aurelie seated on a

porch swing, her hair sticking out in odd directions and her face rosy from sleep.

Lady ran to her and let Aurelie lift her onto her lap, where she settled, resting her chin on her paws, perfectly content to be held.

Beau leaned against a post and studied the woman and the little dog lying across her thighs. "If you had any doubt, you can now be assured *that* is a lap dog."

Aurelia smoothed a hand over the dog's back. "She probably feels safe for the first time in a while. I'd like to take her to a veterinarian today and have him check her over."

"We can do that," Beau said. "I'm pretty sure there's one here in Bayou Mambaloa."

"I need to check my calendar. I'm pretty sure I have a meeting this afternoon with the CEO of one of the companies we've been monitoring for EPA violations."

"Can you postpone or cancel that meeting? I'm not sure it's safe for you to be out and about."

Aurelie's brow wrinkled. "I refuse to be bullied into stepping back from all the work I've done to ensure the bayou's future. I might be the only person in Louisiana who cares enough to make the tough calls to save the bayou from the ravages of corporate greed or climate change."

Beau gave her a brief nod. "Okay, then. After breakfast, we'll swing by the veterinarian's office and get Lady checked out. I'll call my mother and have her check with Pearson's family to see if they know anything about the dog." His brow dipped. "What if she's just a stray? What do you want to do with her?"

Aurelie stared down at the dog in her lap. "I'm not taking her to a shelter if that's where you're going with this conversation."

Beau dropped to his haunches in front of the pair and scratched the dog behind her ear. "I think you just found your new person, you lucky dog."

Lady blinked several times and then closed her eyes.

"I'll make breakfast." Beau straightened. "How do you like your eggs? And do you want bacon and toast?"

"Over easy and all the above. I'd help, but my hands are full, and my lap is otherwise occupied."

Beau glanced around the clearing where the cottage nestled. It appeared to be peaceful and safe. Experience had proven that appearances could be deceiving. Someone could be in the shadows at the tree line, waiting for an opportunity to pick her off or steal her away.

"I'll cook, but I can't keep an eye on you if you're out here and I'm inside." He tipped his head toward the door. "There's a comfortable sofa in the living room. An added bonus for me is that I can see the living room from the kitchen." He raised his eyebrows. "What do you say? Or you might consider feeding the little rat while I prepare our food."

"That's a good idea." Aurelie gathered Lady into her arms and stood. "Since we're feeding her smaller quantities, it should be more often until she gets used to eating regular meals."

Beau held the door for Aurelie and the dog. Once they were inside, he closed and locked the door, glad she'd decided to come inside while he fixed breakfast.

While Beau cooked eggs, bacon and toast, Aurelie poured a small amount of dog kibble into a bowl and refreshed the water bowl for Lady. "I'll wait to put the food down until we're ready to eat," she said. "That way, Lady can eat while we do."

"Bacon's done, and the eggs are almost ready." Beau used a spatula to lift eggs from the skillet to the waiting plate. "Just waiting on the toast."

Aurelie checked the doggy door in the laundry room and found a lever she could set to lock the door.

Beau carried two plates to the dining table.

Aurelie carried glasses of orange juice.

Beau returned to the kitchen to pour a cup of coffee. "Do you want a cup?" he asked.

"Please." Aurelie carried her cup of coffee and Lady's dog food bowl into the dining room.

Lady ate her dog food while Beau and Aurelie ate their breakfast.

After cleaning his plate, Beau sat back with his cup of coffee, reviewing what he knew about the attacks and the information she'd shared with the sheriff and Remy. "You say your work to preserve the bayou has gotten certain corporations in hot water with the EPA. How so?"

"A couple of businesses claimed they were following the EPA's guidelines for disposal of toxic chemicals generated in their manufacturing process-es." Aurelie laid down her fork and lifted her coffee mug. "One company flat-out lied, and their records were fabricated."

"How do you know that?"

She gave a grim smile. "I got a tip from an insider who knew the truth. He gave me a date and a location in the bayou where the toxic chemicals would be dumped. I rented a boat and made sure I was there to capture the act on video. They came to the same spot the next night. I had an EPA agent and the sheriff for that parish with me that time. They caught them in the act."

"Wait." Beau frowned. "Were you alone the first night?"

Aurelie nodded. "I knew I wouldn't get law enforcement or the EPA to listen unless I had evidence. The video was very convincing."

Beau shoved a hand through his hair, shocked that this woman had gone out into the bayou alone, at night, to a location where men were performing an illegal act that could get them thrown into jail. "Were the men dumping the chemicals armed?"

"Yes." She grimaced. "When they tried to escape,

the sheriff had two other boats nearby to block them from getting away. They exchanged gunfire."

Beau couldn't believe what he was hearing. "They let you go with them? An unarmed woman?"

"I had to show them where to go," she said. "When shit hit the fan, they couldn't let them get away, and they didn't have time to drop me off before pursuing the bad guys."

"You're lucky to be alive," he said solemnly.

"The point is, they caught them," Aurelie said. "In a plea bargain, the men doing the dirty work told the EPA agent everything they needed to know about where the chemicals came from and who'd given the order to dump them in the bayou. They paid a visit to the company and shut them down until they put the process in place to safely handle and dispose of toxic byproducts."

"The man you have a meeting with today...is his company violating EPA guidelines?"

"I won't know until I conduct my investigation." She took a cautious sip of her coffee and swallowed. "I start by looking through their records. If anything jumps out as a red flag, I dig deeper."

"How?" he asked, afraid of her response.

"I observe." She lifted her chin. "Sometimes, I sneak onto their grounds or follow their trucks."

"Oh, babe." Beau shook his head. "No wonder they're after you."

Aurelie frowned. "If they were doing what they

were supposed to, I wouldn't have to go to such extreme measures." She leaned forward. "Don't you see? What they're doing to the bayous is killing them. Maybe even killing the people who live there. If I didn't do anything about it, who would?"

He set his cup on the table and took her hands in his. "You have great intentions, and you obviously care about the bayous and the people. Is it worth your life?"

Her fingers curled around his. "If not me...who?"

"That's a job for the EPA and law enforcement. You shouldn't be sneaking onto corporate grounds. They could get you for trespassing. You could end up in jail."

"True," she said, her brow knitting. "But I'm not trespassing when I follow their people out into the bayou or when I test the bayou waters near their facilities."

"I realize saving the bayou is your father's philanthropy, but with you going the extra lengths, are you helping his cause or hurting it?"

"How can it hurt the cause if we stop companies from poisoning the bayou?"

"You said yourself that sometimes the EPA forces the companies to shut down until they put measures in place to clean up their acts." He squeezed her hands gently. "That puts people out of work. When people don't have work, they don't have money to feed their families. They're less likely to care about saving the bayou and more likely to back whoever keeps the factories open."

"Jacob Gousman," she whispered. "My work to save the bayou could cost my father the election."

Beau nodded.

She stared at their joined hands. "I need to back off my investigations until after the election."

"Is that what this afternoon's meeting is about?"

She nodded. "I'm going to talk to Patrick Holzhauer at JBK Chemicals. I got a tip from an anonymous informant that they're not reporting all their industrial waste."

"What do you hope to gain by speaking with him?"

"Maybe an explanation. I don't know who my informant is. He could be wrong."

"Have you received tips from this guy before?"

She nodded.

"Has his information been accurate each time?"

Again, she nodded.

Beau sighed. "You're going to talk to Holzhauer despite almost being killed, aren't you?"

She nodded. "At the very least, I hope to encourage him to leave the world a better place than he found it. For his children. For the future."

"I'm going with you."

She chewed on her bottom lip for a moment. "I set up the appointment in my name only. It's a secure facility. All persons entering their complex are required to submit their names at least a day in advance so they can conduct a background check."

"Call them." Beau said. "Tell them that, based on a recent attack, you're bringing your bodyguard."

Aurelie met his gaze. "Okay." She pulled her hands free of his, rose and walked into the living room where she'd left her cell phone on an end table.

Lady, having finished her food, trotted along behind her.

Beau smiled at the picture they made.

Aurelie returned a few minutes later. "Done. Your name is on their guest list."

"Good, because if they wouldn't let me in, I'd have to raise some hell."

Her lips turned upward. "I would've paid good money to see how that went down."

Beau and Aurelie gathered their dishes and entered the kitchen together. He washed, she dried. They stood so close that their shoulders bumped against each other, making Beau want to pick up where they'd left off before the invasion of the matted mop now named Lady.

Lady stood by Aurelie's feet as if afraid she'd disappear and abandon her.

"I'll need a few minutes to pull myself together," Aurelie said.

"I'll call my mother," Beau said, "and let her know about Lady."

Aurelie's gaze met his.

He cupped her cheek in his palm and brushed a kiss across her lips. "Don't worry. I'll let her know that you'll take her if the family isn't interested."

"I'll take her, even if they are interested," she murmured. "I'll give her a good home."

"I'll let my mother know how you feel. She's an excellent negotiator."

Aurelie grabbed her gym bag and entered the bathroom. She waited for Lady to follow and then closed the door.

Beau dressed quickly in black jeans and a black polo shirt, aiming for the bodyguard vibe. He had a pair of mirrored sunglasses in his truck to add to the look.

With Aurelie still in the bathroom, he grabbed his cell phone and stepped out onto the back porch, leaving the door open so that he could listen for Aurelie.

The first call was to his mother.

"Beau, sweetheart. How was your night in da cottage?"

"Interesting," he answered.

"Oh. Tell me."

He skipped the part about making love with Aurelie and got straight to the home invader, Lady.

"A small white dog, you say?" His mother paused. "I seem to recall Myra Pearson carried a little white dog wit' her everywhere before she died a year ago. I hadn't t'ought about it since den. It could be hers. I'll contact da family and ask what dey want to do wit' it."

"*Maman*, while you're talking with them, ask them what they want for this place, as is."

"Do you know someone interested in buying it da way it is?" she asked.

"Yes, ma'am." The idea had barely taken root in the back of his mind. Now, it was firmly embedded. He'd wanted a place of his own with acreage and preferably on the water. So, it needed work. He wasn't afraid of that. "Maman," he said. "Tell them your buyer wants the dog with the house. Non-negotiable."

"Da dog?"

He hadn't been sure about his reason for surviving. He hadn't been sure he would ever fit into civilian life. But he was sure about this. "Yes, ma'am. The dog."

Another call came in on his cell phone. He glanced at the caller ID. Remy Montagne.

"I have another call coming in I need to take."

"I have what I need," his mother said. "I love you, son. Glad you're home."

He ended the call with his mother and accepted the call from Remy. "Boyette speaking."

"Just heard from the sheriff in Bayou Miste," Remy said. "They got a match on the fingerprints found in Miss Anderson's home."

"Anyone we know?" Beau asked.

"Not unless you're familiar with Cajun mafia hitmen."

Beau's gut clenched. "No shit?"

"No shit," Remy confirmed. "Big Johnny Lansky. He's the primary suspect in a number of execution-style murders."

"Why's he still running loose?" Beau asked.

"They can't come up with sufficient evidence or keep witnesses alive long enough to take him to court," Remy said.

The knot in Beau's gut tightened. "And he was in Aurelie's cottage. Did they find anything on the video footage from the château?"

"Yeah." Remy's tone didn't bode well. What could be worse than having Johnny Lansky after Aurelie?

"Were they able to identify the man in black who attacked Aurelie?"

"Yeah. Ever heard of Slash Duon?"

Beau's stomach roiled. "Fuck."

"Right?" Remy continued. "He was at the masquerade ball. They identified him by the dragon tattoo on his left hand."

"How the hell did he get in?"

"They figure his ticket was purchased under the name of a recognizable donor, and he had an ID made to match."

"So much for security." Beau shoved a hand through his hair. "He was in the ballroom and probably followed Aurelie when she left the building." He was still kicking himself for not sticking with her when she'd gone down the hallway leading to the bathrooms.

A goddamn hitman. He could easily have stabbed her, snapped her neck or shot her before tossing her into the bayou.

"As soon as I heard those two names," Remy was saying, "I passed them to Swede. He's been running background checks on some of the corporate talking heads Miss Anderson met with in her efforts to protect the bayous. He didn't find much on the internet, but when he took the names to the dark web, he found images of some of her CEOs at parties in New Orleans."

"By chance, was Patrick Holzhauer at JBK Chemicals one of those CEOs?" he asked.

"As a matter of fact, yes," Remy said.

Beau braced himself, knowing the parties weren't what was important so much as who was there with the CEOs.

"Here's the thing," Remy said. "In each of the images, the different CEOs were with Manny Marceaux."

"As in the Cajun Mafia kingpin, Manny Marceaux?" Beau breathed in and back out. "When I was a kid, my father told us stories about the Marceaux family in New Orleans. He warned us that whatever we did, stay away from them. And Manny was the worst of them. What is he...in his seventies now?"

"Rumors on the dark web say he's got cancer," Remy said. "Some think he's making a big push to get as many of his people in place as he can before he dies to make sure the family carries on, even without him to lead them."

Beau shook his head. "Then what's his end game? Why pick on a bayou activist?"

"She's causing problems with the people he has in place. Maybe he's getting kickbacks from the companies."

"And when the EPA shuts them down, they don't have money for payola?" Beau paced the length of the porch and back. "Still, she can't warrant two of his best hitmen."

"Sorry, buddy," Remy said. "Your client hit the jackpot on the best of the worst. Do you want me to send backup?"

"Yes." Beau groaned. Aurelie was already chafing at having him running interference. "No. At least not yet. Let me bring Aurelie up to date and let her get used to the idea before we overwhelm her."

"Will do," Remy said. "But don't wait too long to ask for reinforcements."

"Roger."

"Out here." Remy ended the call.

Beau stared out at the bayou, the water so still it reflected the puffs of white clouds drifting overhead.

"Fuck," he muttered and turned to find Aurelie standing in the doorway, dressed in navy slacks, a white silk blouse and black heels. She'd pulled her dark hair back into a neat bun at the nape of her neck. She'd applied makeup that accentuated her beautiful brown eyes and a dark red lipstick.

She held Lady in her arms, a frown denting her forehead. "What's wrong?"

Where did he begin?

"I think you should cancel that meeting with Holzhauer."

"Why?" she asked. When he hesitated, her lips pressed into a thin line. "I have a feeling I'm not going to like this."

"I know you're not going to like what I have to say." He hooked her arm and led her into the house, closing and locking the back door. "Let's get Lady to the vet. I'll fill you in on the way." He didn't stop until he had her out the front door and locked it securely, although hitmen like Lansky and Slash wouldn't let a little thing like a door lock stop them. It wouldn't even slow them down.

By the time they reached the vet's office, Aurelie sat perfectly still in the passenger seat, still holding Lady, stroking her in short, jerky motions.

"Two hitmen," she whispered. "You'd think I'd killed one of the Marceaux family to warrant *two* hitmen." She looked across the console, meeting his gaze. "All because they don't want me to protect the bayou?" She shook her head. "It doesn't make sense. I'm nobody in the grand scheme of things."

"Apparently, you're somebody who threatens the Cajun Mafia." He slid out of his seat, rounded the truck to her door and helped her to the ground.

Aurelie clutched the little dog in her arms. "As much as I don't want to be bullied into stepping back from my one-on-ones with the CEOs of the companies with the worst track records with the EPA," she started, "I think you're right."

Beau cupped her elbow and walked with her toward the entrance of the vet clinic. "Right about what?"

"I'm going to postpone my meeting with Holzhauer," she said as he held the door for her. "Anything I have to say to him will be trumped by whatever hold Manny Marceaux has on him." She walked into the clinic and stepped up to the counter.

Once the receptionist took her information, she sat beside Beau as they waited to be called into an examination room.

Less than a minute later, a vet tech led them into a room with a stainless-steel examination table and two plastic chairs against the wall.

Lady shivered so violently in Aurelie's arms that Beau feared she'd rattle some bones loose.

The veterinarian entered. A tall man with an average build, he smiled and asked why they'd brought the dog in.

Aurelie told him about Lady, who had appeared matted and hungry in the kitchen of the house they were renting.

"Do you know how long she's been on her own? May I?" The vet took Lady from Aurelie and checked her over from nose to tail.

"The man who owned the house died a couple of months ago. She could've been overlooked by the people who discovered the man's body, or she could've been grieving for the old man and ran scared into the woods." Aurelie shrugged. "Is she going to be okay?"

"Other than a few fleas and a little razor burn, she appears to be fine. Without a stool sample, I can't check for worms. Given the fact she's been living in the woods, possibly subsisting on bugs and vegetation, I'm inclined to put her on a flea and tick deterrent, de-worming medication, an antibiotic to take care of anything she might have picked up and a nutritional supplement until she puts on a little weight."

The vet handed Lady to Aurelie. "She appears to have held her own in the wild. A few weeks of healthy food, lots of cuddles and she'll be fine."

They picked up the medications at the reception desk and added a bag full of dog treats. Beau paid the bill.

The vet reappeared. "You know, we should run

the microchip reader and see if we can locate her owner." He nodded to the receptionist.

She rummaged in the desk and pulled out a reader, turned it on and handed it to the vet.

The vet ran the reader over Lady, moving slowly until a number appeared. "Ah," he said. "She does have a microchip. Let me see if we can locate the chip company and find the owner."

The veterinarian sat at a computer terminal and entered the number in a registry database.

Aurelie held Lady, stroking her fur, her brow wrinkled.

Beau slipped an arm around her waist, holding Aurelie lightly, knowing she was already attached to the dog.

"Here it is," the vet said. "The dog belongs to Robbie and Myra Pearson. Do you want the phone number so you can call and let them know their dog has been found?"

"That won't be necessary," Beau said. "The dog's owners are deceased."

The vet frowned. "I'm sorry. Would you and your wife like me to take the dog and turn it over to a shelter?"

Aurelie half-turned away, shielding Lady. "No."

The vet smiled. "If you're keeping her, you'll want to get in touch with the microchip company and have them change the contact information in case the dog gets lost again."

"We will," Beau took the bag of medications and left with Aurelie.

Once out in the truck, he turned to her. "What now?"

She stared at the vet clinic. "I don't know. I feel like I should be meeting with my team, working on ad campaigns and lining up interviews with local celebrities to get their buy-in for saving our natural resources." Aurelie turned to Beau. "But right now, I just can't. All I want to do is hole up in the cottage. Out of sight." Her brow furrowed. "Two hitmen? Wow. I guess I should feel special." She snorted. "All I want to do is what Lady did and disappear into the woods."

Beau's heart pinched hard in his chest. He wanted to make the world right again for Aurelie. The only way he could help would be to take out two hitmen and the leader of the Cajun mafia. How difficult would that be?

CHAPTER 13

LADY SETTLED on Aurelie's lap and fell asleep for the short ride back to the cottage.

Aurelie tried to look at the bright side of the day so far. They'd determined Lady had belonged to the Pearsons. She was as healthy as a dog could be that had been running wild for the past couple of months, foraging on whatever she could find to survive. And she hadn't been eaten by an alligator, coyote or larger dogs.

They had medicines to help her regain her health and were taking her back to the only home she'd ever known.

Aurelie found it helped to focus on someone else other than herself. It was pointless fixating on the fact she had a target on her back with experienced hitmen taking aim.

Caring for Lady helped. But how much of an effort would it be if the dog slept all day?

Aurelie needed to keep moving. She needed a task to occupy her mind, or she'd fall down the rabbit hole of what-ifs.

Beau parked his truck behind the house. "Just in case someone comes looking for us, it won't be as obvious that we're here," he said.

He'd carried his handgun in the console of his truck on the drive to and from town. As soon as he parked, he took it out of the console and tucked it into the waistband of his jeans.

"Isn't that awkward?" Aurelie asked.

He nodded. "Yeah. I've got a shoulder holster in my backpack I plan to wear now that we're here." He helped her to the ground and walked with her up the porch steps. After he unlocked the door, he stepped inside and waited for her to enter. He closed the door and flipped the lever for the deadbolt.

"You know the drill," he stated.

She nodded. "Stay just inside the door while you run a security check."

Beau nodded and winked. "I'll be right back. Don't go anywhere."

Aurelie stood still, following the sound of Beau's footsteps as he moved from room to room. He came back with a smile.

"Let me guess," she said with one eyebrow cocked. "All clear?"

"Yes, ma'am," he said with a grin.

She set Lady on the floor.

The dog raced toward the kitchen where Aurelie had left a bowl of water on the floor earlier.

Aurelie's gaze followed Lady until she disappeared around a corner.

Beau laughed. "I think she feels safe."

"Agreed." She shifted her gaze to meet Beau's. "I can't just sit around waiting for something to happen. Your mother said we could earn our rent by sorting through the Pearson's belongings."

"She did say that." Beau walked with her into the living room and stood looking around. "Do you want to tackle it today?"

She laughed. "It'll take more than a day, but yes. I need to keep busy. Sorting and boxing would give me something productive to do, and staying here at the cottage will make your job of keeping up with me easier." She gave him a crooked grin. "It's a win for both of us."

He clapped his hands together. "I'm in. I think I saw a stack of empty boxes in one of the bedrooms."

They started by labeling three separate boxes as Donate, Family and Trash and went to work in the spare bedrooms first.

They worked all morning, making it through the two bedrooms by noon, stopping several times to pet Lady or to take her outside for short walks on a leash. She was content to sleep most of the day on the living room sofa.

Beau heated leftover gumbo for lunch. They ate on the back porch, enjoying being outside until the heat and humidity drove them indoors to crank up the window air-conditioning units.

They spent the afternoon going through the kitchen and pantry, taking a little longer while sorting through things they could use while they were there.

By late afternoon, they made it to the laundry room and found an attic entrance in the ceiling with stairs that dropped down.

Beau climbed up to get an idea of how much had been stored up there.

When he let out a long, slow whistle, Aurelie groaned. "A lot?"

"Too much to start on today." He backed down the ladder and raised the staircase, folding it up into the ceiling. "More gumbo for dinner, or do you want me to make omelets?"

"Omelets," Aurelie said. "Are we done for the day?"

"I am if you are," he said.

"I'm done." Aurelie led the way out of the laundry room and into the living room, now crowded with boxes stacked against one wall. "That's a lot of stuff. The trash alone will take several trips to the landfill in your truck."

"Or we can have a roll-on, roll-off container delivered. We still have the attic and a storage shed to clear out."

She collapsed onto the sofa and put her feet up on a box labeled FAMILY. Lady rose from her corner of the sofa and climbed onto Aurelie's lap.

"Hey, little Lady," Aurelie crooned. "Need a little lovin'?"

"I'm going to make those omelets. We can eat out here rather than at the dining table." He headed for the kitchen.

"A good idea since it's covered with boxes," Aurelie called out. "Let me know if you need help."

"I've got this," he responded.

"Good, because now that I'm down, I don't think I can get up again."

"Relax." He appeared a moment later with a glass of wine. "This might help."

"Mmm. A man after my own heart. I could get used to being waited on. Just give me wine and chocolate bonbons, and I'm a happy camper."

"I'll be sure to load up on chocolate bonbons next time we go grocery shopping." He winked and headed back to the kitchen.

Aurelie sipped her wine and looked around at all the work they'd done so far. With the pictures removed from the walls and the clutter stored in boxes to be donated or trashed, she could see the potential of the room.

Beau appeared with two plates. He handed one to her and laid the other on a box. "Need a refill on the wine?" he asked.

"I still have enough in this glass," she said.

He returned to the kitchen and came back with another glass of wine and salt and pepper shakers. As he sank onto the sofa beside her, he reached for his plate on the box in front of him and dug into the omelet.

Aurelie was a few bites ahead of him. "I'm starting to see the potential in this cottage."

"Potential?" he asked.

Aurelie pointed to the wall he'd just had to walk around from the kitchen. "If that's not a load-bearing wall, I'd open it up between the kitchen and living room."

Beau nodded. "I like the idea of an open-concept living space. What else?"

"This house has only one bathroom for three bedrooms." She shook her head, her brow puckered. "I'd add an ensuite bathroom to the master bedroom. It would be an owner oasis with a walk-in shower, soaker tub and his-and-hers vanities." She grimaced. "Can you tell I watch a lot of home makeover shows?"

"That's not a bad thing. They have some great ideas."

"You watch them, too?" she asked.

"I did when I was in rehab for my leg." He took a

bite of his omelet, chewed thoughtfully and then swallowed. "You'd open up the living room and add a bathroom. Is that all you'd do?"

Aurelie smiled. "It would be a good start to making this place a home."

"Are you planning major renovations to your place in Bayou Miste?"

Aurelie's lips pressed together. "I don't know. I'm not in a hurry to go back. Knowing a hitman slashed my mattress makes me leery of ever sleeping there again."

"You don't have to worry about it for a while. You could stay here until they sell the place."

She looked around the living room. "I do like the high ceilings and big windows. Fresh paint would brighten it.

They finished their omelets and shared the responsibility of cleaning up the dishes and the kitchen.

"You can have the first shower," Aurelie said, suddenly shy with the man she'd made love with the night before. He hadn't made a move for a repeat of the intimacy they'd shared. Aurelie was beginning to wonder if he'd found her boring.

"You could join me," he said and held out his hand.

Her heart took flight, her pulse shooting blood through her veins as she walked toward the bathroom with him.

He paused at his backpack to retrieve protection and then continued into the bathroom, where he turned on the shower to let the water warm.

They took turns stripping items of clothing off each other until they stood naked on the cool tile floor.

Beau's gaze swept over her, burning in its intensity. "You're so beautiful."

"So are you." She reached out and laid her hand on his broad chest, amazed at how solid he was and how safe she felt with him.

He grinned. "I prefer handsome, but beautiful isn't bad." Beau raised her hand from his chest to his lips, pressing a kiss into her palm. Then he stepped into the shower, drawing her in with him.

Warm water rained down on them as they made love beneath the spray, taking the time to explore while washing away the dust of their day's work.

She took the condom packet off the ledge where Beau had placed it, tore it open and smoothed it over his rock-hard cock, taking her time to reach the base.

As soon as it was in place, Beau lifted her by the backs of her thighs.

Aurelie wrapped her legs around him as he pressed her back against the cool tiles lining the shower wall. The chill of the tile did nothing to douse the inferno burning at her core. This man inspired the heat and fanned the flames spreading throughout her body.

He drove into her until he was fully seated, giving her a few brief moments to adjust to his size. Then he moved in and out, slowly at first, gathering speed with each thrust.

She braced her hands on his shoulders and rode him hard, her thighs clamped around his waist, her breasts rubbing against his chest.

The faster he pumped, the higher she rose until she burst over the edge of her release.

Beau continued to move in and out of her until his body tensed, and he thrust deep, pinning her to the wall as his cock pulsed inside her.

He leaned his forehead against hers until the pulsing of his release subsided, and his breathing returned to normal. Lifting her off his shaft, he lowered her to the shower floor and cupped her cheek. "You make me glad I'm alive," he whispered against her lips and then kissed her gently as if worshipping her mouth.

Something about his words struck her square in her gut. She looked up into his face. "Was there a time you weren't glad you were alive?"

Beau didn't respond. The haunted look in his eyes made Aurelie's heart wrench. She didn't want to spoil the afterglow of their lovemaking, but she wanted to know why he hadn't been glad to be alive. She sensed it was an important part of who he was.

She remembered Benjamin commenting on a crash.

Aurelie met and held Beau's gaze as she reached up to cup his cheek in her hand. "Did it have to do with the crash?"

The shadows around his eyes deepened. "The water's getting cold." He reached around her, turned off the water and stepped out of the shower.

She followed, intent on wrapping her arms around him in an attempt to ease his sadness.

Aurelie was brought up short when his arm shot out, shoving a towel in front of her.

When she took the towel, he stepped out of reach, quickly dried himself and left the bathroom. He headed for his backpack, extracted shorts and a T-shirt, and disappeared down the hallway to the living room.

The heat of their passion was effectively extinguished by Beau's icy withdrawal.

For a moment, Aurelie stared at the empty hallway. A less stubborn woman would have given the man his space.

They didn't call Aurelie her father's daughter for nothing. When an Anderson wanted answers, he or she went after them. Fiercely. Relentlessly.

She dried, grabbed an oversized T-shirt and pulled it over her head. The hem fell to the middle of her thighs, covering enough.

She ran to the living room.

Beau sat on the floor, staring straight ahead with Lady curled up in his lap.

Aurelie lowered herself to sit beside him. She reached for his hand and held it in hers.

For a long time, neither spoke.

Just when she thought Beau might have fallen asleep, he said, "Everyone died."

She froze, not wanting to move even a fraction of an inch and stop the flow of Beau's words.

"Everyone but me," he said so softly she wasn't sure she'd heard him correctly.

She didn't comment, and she certainly didn't judge. She just held his hand while he unburdened his conscience.

"I was last in the chopper and was struggling to secure my harness when a mortar round blew through the fuselage into the cockpit. We weren't more than twenty feet from the ground when it happened. The round exploded. My next memory was waking up in a field hospital, the lone survivor of the crash."

Aurelie's chest was so tight she could barely breathe.

"Everyone died in that helicopter," he whispered.

"Except me," she said, lost in the memory of waking up in the hospital, crying out for her mother, only to be told she was dead.

How long they sat on that floor, Aurelie had no idea. She leaned against his shoulder, taking comfort in his strength and knowing she wasn't alone in her guilt. She truly believed she should have died when her mother had.

Beau stirred beside her. "We're a pair. We make passionate love and then sit staring at nothing, feeling sorry for ourselves." Setting the dog on the floor, he pushed to his feet and reached for her hand. "The least we can do is get some rest so we can do this again tomorrow."

When he held out his hand, she gripped it and let him pull her to her feet. She wrapped her arms around his waist and rested her cheek against his chest. "I'm glad you took the job," she said.

His arms rose up around her. "Me, too. Come on, let's get a real night's sleep in a bed."

They walked into the bedroom and climbed into the bed.

Beau pulled Aurelie into his arms.

She rested her cheek on his chest, listening to the steady beat of his heart. "If you had died in that helicopter...I would have died in the bayou." She tipped her head up to meet his gaze. "You had to live to save me."

"And you had to live so I could save you, thus saving myself." He laughed. "We must be tired. We're not making sense."

"We're making the most sense right now," she argued.

A high-pitched yelp sounded from the floor beside the bed.

Aurelie leaned over the side and reached for the little dog.

Lady moved out of reach, heading for the door.

Aurelie sat up. "She needs to go outside."

"I'll take her." Beau rolled out of the bed and followed the dog out of the room.

Aurelie laid back. No sooner had she closed her eyes than her cell phone chirped, indicating an incoming text.

She reached for it on the nightstand and stared at the message.

All thoughts of sleep flew out the window. Aurelie leaped out of bed and dressed quickly. She was tying the laces on her running shoes when Beau returned, carrying Lady.

He frowned when he saw that she was fully dressed. "Going somewhere?"

She looked up. "My informer just sent me a message. JBK Chemicals is dumping a dozen barrels of industrial waste into the bayou tonight at midnight."

He shook his head. "You're not going out there, are you?"

Aurelie finished tying her lace and stood. "I have to. Someone has to document what they're doing."

"Call the EPA." Beau gripped her arms. "It's their job to police the disposal of hazardous waste, not yours."

"They won't come unless they have evidence." She

met his gaze and held it. "I promise not to get too close. They won't see me."

"How do you know where they'll be?"

"My informant sent me the GPS coordinates."

"And how do you propose to get there?"

"Mr. Pearson's skiff?" She glanced at the clock on the nightstand. "I have to go. I need to make sure the skiff has enough fuel to get me there and back, and I need time to get there early so I can lie in wait for the bastards to arrive."

"You can't do this," Beau said. "It's too dangerous. Lansky and Slash are out there somewhere, waiting for an opportunity to finish the job."

She stared up into his eyes. "This is what I do. It's my purpose, the reason I lived through the crash that killed my mother. I lived to make a difference." She lifted her chin. "I'm going. With or without you."

"I can't protect you if you're halfway across the bayou. Fuck," he muttered. "I'm going with you."

Aurelie nodded. "We have to hurry. It's almost midnight."

CHAPTER 14

PEARSON'S SKIFF appeared seaworthy enough, but it was secured to the dock with a cable and a combination lock. With no way of knowing the correct code, Beau searched the storage shed for something to cut the cable. After digging through an unorganized array of tools, he found a set of bolt cutters and hurried back to the dock to cut through the cable.

That was just the beginning of their challenges.

The small outboard engine attached to the skiff was old and oily. Beau shined a light into the fuel tank. It was as near to empty as it could be without being bone-dry.

He remembered seeing a five-gallon gas can in the shed, hurried back and lifted it, breathing a sigh as liquid sloshed inside it. The gas can was full. He found a bottle of stabilizer on a shelf nearby and grabbed it, too. Pearson might not have used the boat in months, possibly years.

Beau emerged from the shed into the night air. "Aurelie?"

"Coming," she called out, her voice coming from inside the shed. She stepped out, carrying two dark green life jackets. "Thought we might need these."

When they returned to the dock, Beau climbed into the skiff and poured the gasoline into the fuel tank.

Aurelie dropped the life jackets on the floor of the skiff and climbed aboard.

Beau glanced up briefly. "Will Lady be all right on her own?"

Aurelie's brow dipped low. "I didn't like leaving her. She probably thinks she's been abandoned again. I heard her howling and scratching at the laundry room doggy door as I walked away."

"You secured it so that she couldn't get out?"

"I did," Aurelie said. "She was very unhappy."

"It's better that she stay here."

"I know," Aurelie said.

Balancing the gas can with one hand, he dug into his pocket and pulled out his cell phone. "Here," he said, handing it to her. "Call Remy and put him on speaker."

She found Remy's number at the top of his favorites and placed the call, setting the sound on speaker.

Remy answered on the first ring. "Ready for that backup?"

"Yes." Beau filled him in on the text Aurelie had received. "You already have the trace option on my cell phone. Get someone out on the water ASAP. Have them follow but keep a distance. We're heading in to set up before midnight."

"Do you want me to send someone over to protect Miss Anderson at the cottage so you can go to the location alone?" Remy suggested. "Or we can send someone else and leave you and Miss Anderson at the safe house."

Aurelie shook her head. "My informant trusted me with the information. I won't let him down. I'm going."

"Okay, then," Remy said. "I'll gather a couple of our guys and see you out there."

"You're coming?" Beau asked.

"Besides you, I'm the most familiar with navigating Bayou Mambaloa. I'll get right on it. Out here."

Beau was relieved Remy would be one of the men who would have back. The Navy SEAL was a highly trained combatant and a seasoned Cajun.

When the fuel tank was full, Beau set the gas can on the dock, then added stabilizer and screwed the cap on.

Gripping the plastic handle tightly, he pulled the cord. The engine rumbled and died.

He looked for a way to prime it, found a squeeze

bulb and squeezed it several times before trying again.

When he yanked the cord, the engine turned over once and died again.

On his third attempt, the engine rumbled, coughed and then roared to life, belching oily smoke for the first minute.

Aurelie handed him one of the life jackets. "Put this on." She already had the other one on and had taken a seat on the middle metal bench, facing him.

Beau patted the gun he'd stowed in his shoulder holster along with an extra magazine full of rounds. He slid his arms into the vest and buckled the straps, checking to ensure he could still reach his pistol. It was a stretch but doable.

Aurelie leaned over to untie the lead from the post on the dock.

They only had fifteen minutes to get to the coordinates and find a suitable vantage point before midnight. If they didn't get going, they wouldn't have the lead they needed.

He slowly backed the skiff.

As he reached the end of the pier, a flash of white raced across the dock, flew through the air and landed in Aurelie's arms.

"Lady!" she cried out. "How the hell did you get out of the house?"

The dog licked her face, her tail wagging her entire body.

"We can't take her," Beau said.

"We don't have time to take her back to the house." Aurelie met Beau's gaze in the starlight. "I won't leave her on the dock."

Beau hesitated for one second, then whipped the little boat around. Using his cell phone's GPS, he pushed the little skiff as fast as it would go, aware of the time they had left and the distance they needed to cover.

Fifteen minutes until midnight, as they neared the coordinates, Aurelie's cell phone chirped softly. She stared down at the screen and gasped. "Turn back!" she yelled over the sound of the engine. "Turn back now! It's a setup."

"Hold on!" Beau goosed the throttle, turning the rudder at the same time to send the little skiff into a tight spin. He almost tipped it up on edge in his attempt to reverse course.

Before the little boat could right itself, a larger boat slammed into its underbelly, flipping it into the air and slinging its occupants overboard.

Beau plunged into the inky waters of the bayou. He wasn't under long before his life jacket brought him to the surface.

The boat that had hit them turned and raced toward Beau and the overturned skiff.

Beau couldn't swim out of the way fast enough. His only option was to go down. He fumbled for the buckle on his life jacket, pinched it loose and slid his arms out. As the sleek black bass boat powered toward him, he caught a glimpse of the lettering on the front, then dove deep beneath the surface.

The heavy engines roared over his head, missing him by a narrow margin.

Beau swam to the surface as the bass boat skimmed to a stop.

A big guy, matching the same build as the man who'd tossed Aurelie into the bayou, reached over the side, grabbed Aurelie by her life jacket and hauled her into the boat.

No!

Beau kicked hard in an attempt to swim for the bass boat.

A man yelled. "There he is!"

The next moment, bullets pelted the water around him.

Beau dove beneath the surface and swam away from his position before resurfacing in the shadow of the overturned skiff.

The bass boat circled the area where he'd been, a man firing a military-grade rifle into the water.

Beau counted four men and the driver. The lump on the deck had to be Aurelie.

Treading water, Beau pulled his handgun from the holster and aimed at the man with the rifle.

When he pulled the trigger, nothing happened. Even if he could swim fast enough to reach the bass boat, he was one man against five.

His hopes sank to the bottom of the bayou as the bass boat turned and sped away with the woman he loved.

Loved?

Was he in love?

How could he have fallen so fast?

Because she was smart, loyal, beautiful and cared about her family, her state and the bayou. So much so that she put her life in danger to save it.

Whether or not he loved the woman, Beau had failed to protect her. He prayed they wouldn't kill her immediately, that they'd give him enough time to rally his forces and get to her before it was too late.

This couldn't be the end. They were only just beginning.

A whining sound echoed from beneath the overturned skiff.

Lady!

Beau dove under the side of the skiff and surfaced in the pitch-black air pocket.

The sound of little paws desperately paddling in the water made him reach out into the darkness for the little dog Aurelie had grown so attached to.

Beau's fingers encountered a floppy, wet ear. He grabbed it and pulled the animal toward him and into one arm.

Lady clawed at his shoulder, trying to get out of the water.

"Hey," Beau spoke to the pup. "It's okay. You're

going to be all right. Help is on the way." At least, he hoped it was.

Kicking his feet to keep his head above water, Beau pulled his cell phone out of his pocket and clicked the button on the side.

Nothing. Which meant it no longer emitted a signal.

Remy was smart. He'd know to aim for the last location the finder app had located Beau's phone.

Beau just had to stay afloat and not attract the attention of any resident alligators.

For the next few minutes, he remained in the air pocket beneath the skiff.

If Remy had mobilized soon after hanging up with Beau, he'd be on the bayou by now, making his way toward Beau.

When he arrived at the last location the app had seen Beau's phone, Remy and his crew would see the skiff and look for the bodies.

Beau would be ready. He'd seen the first four numbers of the boat's registration number following the LA for Louisiana. If he could find the owner, he might find Aurelie. Whatever they did, they had to hurry.

The hum of an engine vibrated through the water, growing louder.

"Sorry about this, kid," Beau said to Lady. Holding her tightly in his arms, he dove down and came back up on the outside of the skiff.

An airboat approached, its massive fan roaring. It slowed as it neared. A floodlight blinked on, shining down on the water's surface.

"Boyette! A voice called out.

Relief flooded through Beau. He raised his free hand. "Over here!"

The beam of light swung toward him, skimming across the water until it found him, blinding him with its intensity.

Beau kicked to keep his head above water, held Lady with one arm and shielded his eyes with the other.

The boat circled and sped toward him. As it neared, the driver kicked into reverse to bring it to a stop within a few feet of Beau and Lady.

Hands reached over the side.

Beau shoved Lady into a pair.

"What the fuck?" Gerard Guidry straightened, holding the wet animal out in front of him.

Lucas and Remy leaned over the side, grasped Beau's wrists and dragged him up onto the deck of an airboat.

"Where's Miss Anderson?" Remy asked.

"They rammed our boat, fished her out of the water and left, firing what appeared to be an AR-15 at me in the water."

Lucas handed him a towel.

Beau dried his hands. "Get Swede on the phone. Now."

Remy pulled his cell phone out of his pocket and called the Brotherhood Protectors computer guru, placing the call on speaker.

Swede answered immediately. "Did you find him?"

"Got Boyette here," Remy said and handed Beau the phone.

"Swede, the boat that rammed us and took Miss Anderson had a Louisiana registration. It was coming at me fast, but I think the numbers after LA were 5031. It's all I got. It was a bass boat, if that helps."

"Got it, running it through Louisiana's DMV database. Hold on."

Beau counted the seconds. The longer it took to find her, the greater the chance they wouldn't get there in time.

Hurry, Swede.

"I have several hits on those numbers. They all belong to the same company. A marina located in a town called—"

He knew before Swede said it. "Bayou Miste?"

"Yeah. That's the one," Swede said. "Thibodeaux Marina."

Beau pulled his phone out of his pocket to call his cousin Ben. He started to punch the buttons when he remembered the phone was dead. He had no way of accessing his contacts. "Swede, give me the cell phone number of Benjamin Boyette."

"I can do one better," Swede said. "Setting up a

three-way call with a Benjamin Boyette of Bayou Miste."

"He might not answer if he doesn't recognize the number," Beau said.

"I have the caller ID set to Brotherhood Protectors," Swede said.

The line rang once. "Ben Boyette speaking."

"Ben, it's Beau. I need your help."

"Name it," Ben said. "Whatever you need, I'm there for you."

"The Cajun mafia have Auri. They're transporting her on one of Thibodeaux's new bass boats."

"Bringing up the tracker app as we speak," Ben said.

A message popped up on Remy's phone, caller ID indicating it was Senator Anderson.

Beau shook his head. "We have an incoming call from Senator Anderson."

"I'll hold," Ben said.

"Holding," Swede said.

Beau pressed the button to hold current calls and answer the incoming one.

"What the hell happened?" Senator Anderson's voice boomed in the night air. "I thought the Brotherhood Protectors had my daughter's protection under control. Then I get a text message. If I don't publicly withdraw my bid for reelection in the next hour, they'll conveniently forget where they left her in the backwaters of the bayou. No one will get to her before alligators do. And if I call in law enforcement, they'll weigh her down with cement and throw her in." The senator sucked in a shaky breath. "At first, I thought it was a joke. Then they sent me a photo of my girl." His voice choked.

Remy's phone chirped in Beau's hand as a text message came through.

Beau brought it up, his heart sinking to the bottom of the bayou.

Auri sat on the bank of the bayou, tied to a tree with a rope, her eyes closed as if she were unconscious or...dead.

Beau enlarged the image, studying her face.

Her cheeks still had a lot of color in them.

She was alive.

Beau clung to that little bit of hope.

"I'm drafting my withdrawal letter," the senator said. "I have an emergency call out to a Baton Rouge news reporter, asking him to meet me in front of my house in thirty minutes. My daughter's life is worth more to me than a political office. I just don't think it will be enough. What if they don't tell us where she is in time?"

"Senator Anderson, Beau Boyette here." He searched for words to reassure this man that his daughter would be okay. Unfortunately, he couldn't guarantee the outcome. Not when they were working against the clock and the men who'd taken Aurelie were brutal killers. "We'll find her."

"Do it. She's all I have." The senator ended the call.

Beau unmuted the other two callers, who were on hold. "Ben?" he said.

"All boats are accounted for at the marina, but one," Ben responded.

"Can we see the path it took through the bayou?" Beau held his breath, praying for the right answer.

"Yes," Ben said. "I've been talking with Swede."

Swede's voice came on the line. "I can set it up for you to see what Ben sees on the tracker app."

Beau's heart swelled with even more hope. "The entire path?"

"Yes, sir," Ben said. "From the moment the boat was rented at Thibodeaux Marina by a James Smith."

"By the way," Swede said. "I ran a check on the driver's license the man used to rent the boat. The man on the license has been dead for a year. Murdered in New Orleans."

"I need that map now," Beau said, "or Miss Anderson will be the next murder victim."

A message came across on Remy's phone. Beau brought it up, clicked on the link and a map filled the screen. "We're in business. Let's find our girl."

CHAPTER 15

AURELIE SLUMPED against the ropes binding her to the tree. When they'd pulled her out of the water, she'd fought hard, kicking, biting and scratching until the big guy she recognized as the man who'd thrown her into the bayou backhanded her so hard she'd passed out. Not for long, but long enough to know she wasn't strong enough to fight her way out of this predicament.

She had to come up with a better plan.

Though she'd regained consciousness, she pretended to still be out cold, using the guise to learn more about her capturers and their plan for her and to come up with her own escape.

When they'd tied her to the tree, she'd let her head loll and her body remain limp. As they'd pushed her back up against the tree, she'd arched it and puffed out her arms like a defensive lineman. They'd tied her body tightly, but when her captors weren't looking, she'd relaxed, and the ropes around her slipped lower.

The men who'd plucked her out of the water stood near the boat they'd used to ram Pearson's skiff.

Aurelie had been conscious when they'd pulled her out and when they'd fired rounds into the water at Beau. She hadn't been able to see him, nor had she seen Lady. Since the men on the boat weren't celebrating the kill, she hoped and prayed Beau and Lady had escaped.

The boat had zigzagged through the bayou, going deeper and deeper into the narrower channels. Trees had hung over the water, making it difficult to see past their branches.

Even if she did escape, Aurelie feared she'd get lost trying to find her way back. As far into the backwaters as they were, Beau and his team would never find her. The phone in her pocket had been submerged and probably wouldn't work. Her prospects were looking grim.

If she weren't her father's daughter, she might've just given up. But she was made of sturdier stuff than that. She'd be damned if she went down without a fight. For the first time since her mother had died, she wasn't weighed down by the guilt that she'd lived when her mother had died in that car wreck.

Being with Beau had been the catharsis she'd

needed to shake free of the regret. Knowing he'd felt the same kind of survivor's guilt had helped her see how foolish it was to wallow in the what-ifs. The people who'd died would have wanted them to live their lives to the fullest, not wish they'd died instead.

Since meeting Beau, Aurelie had discovered an unquenchable desire. For the man, yes. But more importantly...for life. Her guilt had held her back from dreaming of a future filled with hope for a man to love and who would love her. For children. She hadn't allowed herself to consider children. She'd thought she didn't deserve them. Didn't deserve to be happy.

Beau...and Lady had awakened her happy gene, setting her on the path to a future where she could see herself living a full, joyful existence. No longer was she standing in her own way of that goal.

The only thing standing in her way now was the group of men plotting her demise.

Well, fuck them.

She relaxed back against the tree and used her fingers to move the rope around, searching for the knot. Moving her shoulders and her fingers, she worked the loops around until she could feel the knot the men had tied so tightly, now looser like the loops of rope around her.

Maintaining the appearance of being unconscious, she worked her fingers into the knot while listening to the conversation between the men.

The two biggest men had to be Slash and Lansky, the hit men. She didn't understand why they hadn't just shot her like they'd been shooting at Beau. Not that she was disappointed that she was still alive. It just didn't make sense.

Unless the previous attacks had been warnings. Slash could have killed her before throwing her into the bayou. As big as he was, he could easily have snapped her neck, choked her or worse.

The home invasion, care of Lansky, had happened while she'd been at the masquerade ball. Since the two men worked for Manny Marceaux, they had to have planned the simultaneous attacks, knowing exactly where she'd be and when.

The two hitmen were known to her, but who were the other men standing near the boat? She'd bet the man who commanded the attention of all the others was Marceau himself, the Cajun mafia king-pin. It wasn't until the younger man turned enough for the starlight to shine down on his face that Aurelie recognized him and gasped before she could contain her shock.

The five men turned toward the noise.

She kept her head down and tried to look as limp as a ragdoll, with only ropes keeping her from falling over.

"Are you sure she's unconscious?" Jason Gousman asked.

"It doesn't matter if she's unconscious or wide

awake," Marceaux said. "By the time anyone finds her, she'll be little more than scattered bones."

"Then why not kill her now?" the other man asked. "Why leave anything to chance?"

"We hold all our cards until the senator announces his withdrawal from the race," Marceaux said. "He might demand a last-minute proof of life, especially since the last image sent was of his precious little girl unconscious." Marceau glared at Slash. "We need her alive until the announcement goes out on television. That means you don't get to hit her until I tell you to hit her. Got it?"

The big hitman gave a single nod of his head.

"Seems to me you're expending a lot of energy on the wrong person," the mystery man said. "Taking out the whistleblower should keep tree-huggers like her from snooping around where she doesn't belong. She never would've known where to look and when to show up if it hadn't been for the tips she received. I pay you well enough to keep shit like that from happening. What guarantee can you give me that this won't happen to my interests?"

Marceaux stepped up to the other man, getting nose-to-nose with him. "You pay me to do your dirty work. Do you think you can do better? Knock yourself out. You couldn't even keep the snitch from infiltrating your precious company and discovering you don't play by the rules any more than the others the bitch has already had the EPA shut down."

Marceaux's voice lowered to a dangerous rumble. "And remember, you didn't get to where you are without a few skeletons hiding in your closet. Or should I say in the foundation of your new office complex in New Orleans? What's your tagline, again? 'JBX Chemicals built on trust?' How about 'built on the bones of your competitors?'"

"I don't know what you're talking about," the man blustered.

Aurelie finally placed the mystery man. Patrick Holzhauer, CEO of JBX Chemicals. She was supposed to have met with him earlier that day. All the while, he'd been paying Marceaux's Cajun mafia to keep the EPA out of his business.

Had the other corporations she'd exposed quit paying Marceaux to run interference with EPA agents?

And what was Jason Gousman's involvement in the Cajun mafia?

"You think that by ousting Anderson from the senatorial race and putting this puppet of yours in his place, the EPA will stop looking into our activities?"

"He's running on a campaign to bring more business to the state and thus jobs. It's what the voters want. He can legislate looser guidelines, which means cheaper costs of doing business. More companies will flock into the state."

Holzhauer snorted. "More people with jobs to fill your casinos and line your pockets."

"It's a win-win for everyone," Marceaux said.

"I don't like standing around. I don't know why you insisted I come along," Holzhauer said.

"Let's just say the more skin you have in the game, the less likely you'll blab to the feds." Marceaux tipped his head toward Aurelie. "When she dies, you become an accessory to murder—only if you open your mouth."

"So, this is your way of ensuring our silence." Holzhauer turned to Gousman. "You're part of this, as well, about to become a public servant, someone who should be of the highest moral standards."

Gousman snorted. "What politician is?"

Marceaux glanced at his watch. "Anderson has thirty-five minutes to make his announcement. Once he's out of the race, Gousman has no competition."

"And you don't think people will question his sudden withdrawal?" Holzhauer asked.

"Not when the public learns of the disappearance of his only child."

"What will keep him from talking when you don't give him his daughter after doing as you demanded?" Gousman asked.

"Dead men don't talk," Marceaux said. "He'll die of a heart attack. The press will say he died of a broken heart." He turned to Slash. "Get the bucket out of the boat."

Slash went to the boat and came back with a five-gallon bucket.

"It's about to get interesting around here," Marceaux said. He nodded to Slash.

The hitman waded into the water, opened the bucket and dumped it a little at a time, backing out of the water and up the bank toward Aurelie.

She could smell the stench of rotten fish entrails. Her pulse raced when she realized what he was doing.

Slash was chumming the water to lure alligators.

Marceaux's cell phone chirped with an incoming text. "It's done. Anderson just made an announcement on television that he's withdrawing from the race." He looked up. "Our work here is done."

"What about her?" Slash asked.

"No one will find her in time," Marceaux said. "The alligators will take care of the rest."

The five men climbed into the boat and left the island and Aurelie.

She hadn't untangled the knot, she didn't have a way off the island other than to swim—and were those eyes reflecting the starlight, floating just above the water toward the chum...toward her?

Aurelie worked harder to loosen the knot. With an alligator eating its way through the chum and moving closer with each passing second, she didn't have time. Every second mattered, and more floating eyes joined the first pair, all looking for the free meal.

Aurelie vowed that she would not be the next entrée.

.   .   .

"THE TRACKING DEVICE hasn't moved for a while. We're getting closer," Beau said. "It should be less than a quarter mile from here. It has to be where they're holding Aurelie."

"It has to be the place," Lucas said. "I haven't seen any signs along the way that would indicate she's been there."

"Should we slow down, maybe cut the engines and float in silently?" Remy suggested.

Beau resisted the idea. The sooner they got there, the sooner they could rescue Aurelie.

Suddenly, the blue dot moved, heading away from them. "They're on the move."

Remy pushed the throttle forward, increasing the speed.

They curved through narrow channels, ducked beneath low-hanging tree branches and emerged into a small lagoon, nearly ramming into half a dozen alligators, writhing, twisting and fighting over pieces of something floating in the water.

Some of the creatures were on the shore, also eating.

Beau stared in horror. What were they eating?

Remy pulled out a pistol and fired off several rounds, not aiming at anything in particular.

The noise had the desired effect, or they'd run out of whatever they'd been consuming. The half dozen or more alligators slipped into the water and swam away.

Remy ran the front of the airboat up onto the shore and cut the engine. Silence reigned.

"Aurelie!" Beau shouted. *Please don't let us be too late.* "Aurelie!"

"I'm here," a voice called out from somewhere in the branches of a tree.

Beau leaped out and ran for the tree, keeping a wary eye out for more alligators.

When he reached the tree, he peered up into the dark branches. "Hey, babe, are you all right?"

"I am now," she said, dropping to the ground and into his arms. "I wasn't so sure a few minutes ago." She nodded toward the rope wrapped around the tree. "That was too close."

Beau crushed her to him and held her there, remembering how to breathe. "I'm so sorry," he said. "I was supposed to protect you, and I didn't."

"No," she said. "It was my fault. I shouldn't have gone chasing after criminals. And I shouldn't have dragged you along." She cupped his face and kissed him. "I was so worried. I didn't know what had happened to you." She kissed him again. "One minute, I was holding Lady; the next, we were flying through the air. I didn't even see them coming." Her eyes rounded. "Oh my God. Lady!"

A shrill bark sounded from the boat.

Beau slipped an arm around her waist and turned

her toward the airboat. "I found her under the skiff in the air pocket."

Gerard held up Lady, so Aurelie could see the wiggling, squirming little dog.

Aurelie hurried toward her and climbed onto the boat, taking Lady from Gerard. She hugged the dog to her, laughing as she was covered in doggy kisses. "How did you find me?"

"The bass boat has a GPS tracking device on it," Beau said.

Her eyes widened. "Ben's tracking experiment?"

Beau nodded.

Aurelie's eyes narrowed. "So, you can still track it?"

Beau glanced down at the app on his cell phone. The blue dot was still moving. "Yes."

"We have to go after it," she said. "We have to stop them."

Remy took the helm, backed away from the island and turned in the direction the bass boat was heading. "Gerard, text Shelby and let her know what's happening. She's on standby with her people in the sheriff's department. We can have them be there when that boat docks."

"Only if you know where it's going to dock," Aurelia said.

"We're tracking it now." Beau held up Remy's cell phone, displaying the blue dot and the blue path it had taken.

"They could veer off at the last minute and dock somewhere else. It takes a lot longer to change courses on land if you have to drive along a jagged shoreline." She caught Beau's hand. "They baited those alligators and left me to die. We can't let them get away. Slash, Lansky and Marceaux are the ones who were ready to murder me. Marceaux is the one who orchestrated the attacks and forced my father to withdraw from the race so he could put his puppet, Jason Gousman, in place. Patrick Holzhauer was also there."

"That would be an impressive haul to indict all of them for kidnapping and attempted murder," Remy said, yet still hesitated.

"At the very least, follow them. If they get away, they'll claim some bullshit alibi and say I made it all up. Who would believe a senatorial candidate and a bigshot CEO would be hanging out with the Cajun mafia?"

Remy met Beau's gaze. "She's right. We can't let them walk away from this. Marceaux and his hitmen have called the shots for too long. This might be the chance to put them away for good."

Beau nodded. "Just don't get within range of that rifle. Follow. Don't engage."

Remy pushed the throttle all the way forward. The airboat leaped forward, racing through the bayou, weaving through the channels and gradually gaining on the slower bass boat.

Extreme speed wasn't an option with all the twists and turns they had to make. The airboat had an advantage over the bass boat when it came to marshes. It could skim through the tall grasses without fouling propellers.

They emerged into just such a marsh. Starlight lit the marsh well enough that they could see the bass boat weaving through the open channels.

Suddenly, the bass boat leaped forward, speeding away.

"We've been spotted," Remy called out over the fan's roar.

"Don't lose them," Aurelie yelled.

Remy kicked up the speed, racing through the marsh grasses, still gaining ground.

The bass boat aimed for the darker shadows of the bayou with the overhanging trees, probably thinking they'd have a better chance of disappearing into the low-hanging trees where the airboat would be too tall to enter.

Beau held onto his seat with one hand and Aurelie with the other as they bounced across the marsh field. Remy ran parallel with the bass boat, gaining ground until he passed the boat and cut them off from entering the trees.

The bass boat spun to the left and raced for a different entrance.

Before they reached it, another boat appeared out of nowhere and cut off the bass boat, barring it from entering the heavily wooded area of the bayou.

The bass boat spun in a circle and then headed straight for the airboat.

Remy turned and let it chase them until it almost caught up.

Beau saw a stump ahead and shouted, "Watch out!"

With the bass boat so close on their tail, they were headed for disaster.

Beau wrapped his arms tightly around Aurelie and Lady and braced himself.

Seconds away from impact, Remy turned the airboat and hit the throttle, missing the stump by a mere foot.

The bass boat wasn't so lucky. The driver didn't see the stump until too late.

The bass boat hit the huge cypress stump, and the stump split the boat in half, catapulting its occupants. Some slammed into the stump. Others crashed into the debris, sinking beneath the bayou's surface.

Remy circled back and approached the wreckage at the same time as the other boat arrived.

Remy cut the engine on the airboat and glanced across at what turned out to be a sheriff's boat. "About time you got here," he called out.

Remy's fiancé, Deputy Shelby Taylor, eased her boat closer to what was left of the bass boat. "Took a minute for Swede to push the tracking app to my cell phone." The deputy with her shined a spotlight into the water.

Gerard held another spotlight, searching for the passengers.

Beau stood and scanned the dark water. A movement caught his eye at the base of the stump. "There!"

Shelby grabbed a long pole with a shepherd's hook at the end from the side of her boat and positioned it close to the man holding onto the roots of the stump. "Grab the hook," she yelled.

The man batted at the hook until his hand closed around it.

Shelby dragged him through the water to the platform on the back of the boat. The other deputy pulled his gun and aimed it at the man.

"It's Jason Gousman," Aurelie said. "He's unarmed."

The deputy laid down his gun and hauled the man aboard, helping him into a seat.

"Got a live one over here!" Lucas shouted from the front of the airboat.

With the engine off, the airboat wasn't going to get any closer. Beau kicked off his shoes, slid over the side and dropped into the water. He swam toward a man holding onto a piece of the wreckage with one arm. From behind and mostly submerged in the water, he wasn't identifiable.

Beau approached cautiously.

As he came close, the man spun around, bringing the AR-15 rifle around with him.

Beau dove down.

The muffled sound of a shot being fired reached him. He surfaced next to the man, realizing it was Slash, the man who'd thrown Aurelie into the bayou. His eyes were wide open, staring into space. The rifle was gone now.

Beau felt the man's neck for a pulse.

"I shot him. He's dead," Shelby said as she drove her boat up close to where Beau treaded water. "We'll still need to load him into the boat."

After searching for another twenty minutes, they found the other passengers.

"That's all of them," Aurelie said.

All the bodies were loaded onto the sheriff's boat. Jason Gousman sat quietly, shaking and in shock.

They headed for the Bayou Mambaloa marina, where they were met by ambulances and the State Police.

Aurelie used Remy's cell phone to call her father and let him know she was all right. The senator was so relieved he cried. Aurelie cried. Beau's eyes became suspiciously moist as he held her in his arms throughout the call.

News had spread fast that Manny Marceaux was dead. The press arrived, and the marina became a circus.

Beau and Aurelie gave their statements and

contact information and caught a ride with a deputy to the cottage where the night had begun.

Lady entered the house, went straight for her food dish, ate two bites, and lay on the floor beside it.

Beau checked the doggy door she'd managed to open and pushed the trash can in front of it in case she tried to leave in the middle of the night.

When he returned to the living room, Aurelie took his hand, led him into the bathroom and turned on the shower. They peeled off their damp clothing and stepped beneath the spray.

Beau wrapped his arms around Aurelie.

She wrapped her arms around his waist.

They stood in each other's arms for a long time.

"Thank you," Beau whispered.

She shook her head without looking up. "For what?"

"For not dying," he said. "For being the badass you are."

"Thank you for saving me again and for saving Lady."

"There was no other option," he said. "You saved me and gave me a reason to live. Hope for a future. One I want to spend with you."

Her arms tightened around his waist. "Is it possible to fall in love in such a short time?" she whispered. "Because this feels like it."

"I feel like we've been together for a lifetime with all that's happened," he said. "For so long, I didn't know what I wanted. Now, I do. I want you. I want a family. I want to tear out that wall and make this an open-concept living space." He leaned back and tipped her chin up. "Am I scaring you?"

Aurelie laughed. "No, you're making me so happy I can't form words sufficient to express myself." She smiled up at him. "But who needs words when there's always body language?"

Beau claimed her lips and then her body, finally having found his way home.

EPILOGUE

"BEAU! BEAU!" Aurelie stood on the porch of the Old Pearson House she and Beau had purchased together in Bayou Mambaloa. They'd spent their free time over the past two months remodeling. They still had a lot to do, but just opening up the wall between the living room and kitchen had made it feel like a completely different home.

She'd been helping her father with his re-election campaign, with only six more weeks until the election.

When news broke that he had only withdrawn from the race to save his daughter, his polling numbers had skyrocketed, and people campaigned for him to re-enter the race.

Aurelie's testimony to the state police and the EPA helped launch a full investigation into corporations suspected of having ties with the Cajun mafia.

Without Manny Marceaux's leadership, his organization had fractured and weakened, unfortunately spawning gang violence in New Orleans between the warring splinters of what once had been a single organization.

Although it wasn't in Aurelie's nature to wish ill on anyone, she was glad Marceaux and his two hitmen had died in the boat wreck. She didn't feel like she had to keep looking over her shoulder for the next attack.

Jason Gousman dropped out of the senatorial race. Though he was cleared of attempted murder charges, his connection with Marceaux blackballed him with any political organization or major corporations. The last Aurelie heard, he'd moved to Alaska and had gone to work as a night manager for a hotel in Fairbanks.

After dating for two weeks following all the drama, Beau had met with Aurelie's father and asked his permission to marry his daughter.

Her father had told him he'd have to ask Aurelie. She had a mind of her own. They grilled steaks, drank beer and found common ground in their love of fishing.

Aurelie converted her house in Bayou Miste into a vacation rental, not wanting to sever ties with the community she'd just started to love. Beau would make sure that wouldn't happen. They spent time with his cousins at the Raccoon Saloon and had dinner with his aunt and fifteen of her nineteen children.

Lady bounced back from her time as a stray by eating so much she'd turned into a roly-poly chunk. She'd been fine up until that morning.

Aurelie had woken up early, her stomach upset and queasy. She'd blamed it on the cupcake she'd eaten too late the night before. As the morning wore on, her stomach settled, and she worked on moving things out of the guest bedroom. It was the next room they'd paint in their quest to paint every wall in the house.

She'd been working for a couple of hours when she realized she hadn't seen Lady in all that time. Usually, the little dog followed her around the house, sometimes insisting she sit so that she would have a lap to occupy.

Aurelie looked in all of Lady's usual places. She started to worry when she couldn't find her, and the dog didn't come when she called out her name.

Beau emerged from the shed out back where he'd been building shelves and organizing tools.

He climbed the porch steps and pulled Aurelie into his arms, planting a kiss on her lips. "What's up?"

"I can't find Lady."

"Did she unlock the doggy door again?"

Aurelie shook her head. "No. I checked. I looked everywhere I could think she might be and can't find her. I'm worried she somehow slipped out while I wasn't looking."

"Let me look around. She might have found a new place to hide, though how she can hide when she'd such a chunk, I don't know."

"Right?" Aurelie leaned up and kissed her fiancé. "Thanks."

"Anything for my badass woman." He entered the house and went to all the usual places she'd already checked.

Aurelie followed him, her worry growing. "Where could she have gone? Should we look in the woods?"

Beau moved from room to room, looking under beds, in closets and behind chairs.

In the master bedroom, he checked beneath the bed and in his closet and walked into Aurelie's closet. He was closing the door when he paused and went back inside. He parted the row of sweaters and blazers that hung on the lower rod and laughed.

"What?" Aurelie asked, trying to see what he was laughing at.

"I found her," he said and backed out of the closet so Aurelie could enter.

"Is she all right?" she asked as she knelt to look where Beau had been.

Lady was there, lying on her favorite blanket. And she wasn't alone. She had three little puppies, nursing on her teats. Two white ones and one black and white.

Aurelie grinned. "I guess you weren't getting fat after all. Good job, sweet girl. Now we need to figure out who's the father."

As she straightened, Aurelie was struck by a wave of nausea.

She dove for the door, pushing past Beau, her hand over her mouth as she raced for the bathroom, barely making it in time to lose her breakfast over the toilet.

Beau entered the bathroom behind her, grabbed a washcloth from the cabinet, got it wet and handed it to Aurelie. "Hey, are you okay?"

She pressed the cloth to her mouth, already feeling better. "I think it's that cupcake I ate before bed last night. Remind me not to do that again. I was just so hungry."

"Uh, sweetheart," Beau helped her to her feet, "when was your last period?"

She frowned. "Three weeks ago...? That night we had dinner with Ben and Lucy."

"Babe, that was six weeks ago."

She smiled. "I've been so busy, I hadn't noticed." Then his words sank in. "Six weeks? I'm never late." Her eyes widened. "Do you think... Could I be..."

"Pregnant?" He pulled her into his arms. "Would that be a bad thing?"

"Bad?" She shook her head, trying to wrap her mind around this news. "A baby? Bad?" Her face split into a grin. "That's the best news ever!" She flung her arms around his neck and kissed him until they both laughed.

"We might want to push up our wedding date," Beau said.

"What are you doing next weekend?" she asked.

He scooped her up and spun her around. "Getting married next weekend, a baby on the way... Life doesn't get better than this." He set her on her feet. "I'm glad I got the chance."

She smiled up at him. "So am I."

ATHENS AFFAIR

BROTHERHOOD PROTECTORS
INTERNATIONAL BOOK #1

New York Times & USA Today
Bestselling Author

ELLE JAMES

BROTHERHOOD PROTECTORS
INTERNATIONAL

ATHENS AFFAIR

New York Times & USA Today Bestselling Author
ELLE JAMES

CHAPTER 1

Hiring on with the Jordanian camera crew as their interpreter hadn't been all that difficult. With Jasmine Nassar's ability to speak Arabic in a Jordanian dialect and also speak American English fluently, she'd convinced the Jordanian camera crew she had the experience they needed to handle the job. However, the resume she'd created, listing all the films she'd worked on, had probably lent more weight to their decision.

Not that she'd actually worked on any movie sets. Her ability to "be" anything she needed to be, to fit into any character or role, was a talent she exploited whenever needed since she'd been "released" from the Israeli Sayeret Matkal three years earlier.

Her lip curled. Released was the term her commanding officer had used. *Forced out* of the special forces unit was closer to the truth. All because of an affair she'd had with an American while she'd been on holiday in Greece. Because of that week in Athens, her entire life had upended, throwing her into survival mode for herself and one other—her entire reason for being. The reason she was in Jordan about to steal the ancient copper scroll.

The Americans arrived on schedule for the afternoon's shoot at the Jordan Museum in Amman, Jordan. The beautiful film star Sadie McClain appeared with her entourage of makeup specialists, hairstylists, costume coordinators, and a heavy contingent of bodyguards, including her husband, former Navy SEAL Hank Patterson.

Sadie was in Jordan to film an action-adventure movie. All eyes would be on the beautiful blonde, giving Jasmine the distraction she'd need to achieve her goal.

Much like the movie heroine's role, Jasmine was there to retrieve a priceless antique. Only where Sadie was pretending to steal a third-century BC map, Jasmine was there to take the one and only copper scroll ever discovered. The piece dated back to the first century AD, and someone with more money than morals wanted it badly enough he'd engaged Jasmine to attain it for him.

Up until the point in her life when she'd been driven out of her military career, she'd played by the rules, following the ethical and moral codes demanded by her people and her place in the military. Since the day she'd been let go with a dishonorable discharge, she'd done whatever it took to survive.

She'd been a mercenary, bodyguard, private investigator and weapons instructor for civilians wanting to know how to use the guns they'd purchased illegally to protect themselves from terrorist factions like Hamas.

Somewhere along the way, she must have caught the eye of her current puppet master. He'd done his homework and discovered her Achilles heel, then taken that weakness in hand and used it to make her do whatever he wanted her to do.

And she'd do it because he had her by the balls. He held over her head the one thing that would make her do anything, even kill.

Her contact had timed her efforts with the filming of the latest Sadie McClain blockbuster. The museum was closed to the public that afternoon but was filled with actors, makeup artists, cameramen, directors and sound engineers.

The American director had insisted on an interpreter, though Jasmine could have told him it was redundant as nearly half the population of Jordan spoke English. Part of the deal they'd struck with the Jordanian government had been to employ a certain percentage of Jordanian citizens during the production of the movie. An interpreter was a minor concession to the staffing and wouldn't interfere with the rest of the film crew.

Plus, one inconsequential interpreter wouldn't be noticed or missed when she slipped out with the scroll in hand.

For the first hour, she moved around the museum with the film crew, reaffirming the exits, chokepoints and, of course, the location of her target. She'd visited the museum days before as a tourist, slowly strolling through, taking her time to examine everything about the building that she could access, inside and out.

The scroll was kept in a climate-controlled room away from the main hallways and exhibits. Since the facility was closed to the public, there wouldn't be anyone in the room.

While the crew set up for a scene with Sadie McClain, Jasmine slipped into the room to study the display cases once more.

The copper scroll had been cut into multiple pieces. Each piece had its own display case with a glass top, and each was locked. She'd brought a small file in the crossbody satchel she carried, along with a diamond-tipped glass cutter in the event the locks proved difficult. Cutting glass was the last resort. It would take too much time and could make too much noise if the glass shattered.

She'd honed her skills in picking locks and safe-cracking as a child, one of the many skills her mother had taught her. She'd insisted Jasmine be able to survive should anything ever happen to her parents.

Her mother had been orphaned as a small child in the streets of Athens. To survive, she'd learned to steal food and money, or valuables that could be sold for cash or traded for food.

From picking pockets and swiping food from stores and restaurants, she'd worked her way up to stealing jewelry, priceless antiques and works of art from the rich all around the Mediterranean. She'd used her beauty and ability to quickly learn new languages to her advantage, infiltrating elite societal circles to divest the rich and famous of some of their wealth.

She'd gone from a starving, barefoot child, wearing rags in the streets of Athens, to a beautiful young woman, wearing designer clothes and shoes and moving among the who's who of the elite.

Her life had been what she'd made of it until she'd met Jasmine's father, a sexy, Israeli Sayeret Matkal soldier, at an Israeli state dinner attended by wealthy politicians, businessmen and their wives. She'd just stolen a diamond bracelet from the Israeli prime minister's wife.

The special forces soldier outfitted in his formal uniform had caught her with the diamond bracelet in her pocket and made her give it back as if the woman had dropped it accidentally.

Rather than turn her in for the theft, he'd kept her

close throughout the evening, dancing with her and pretending she was just another guest.

Her mother had fallen for the handsome soldier and agreed to meet him the next day for coffee. Less than a month later, they'd married.

For love, her mother had walked away from her life as a thief to be a wife and mother. But she'd never forgotten the hard lessons she'd learned on the streets. She'd insisted her daughter learn skills that could mean the difference between independence and dying of starvation or being reliant on someone who didn't give a damn about her health or happiness.

Her mother had taught her what school hadn't, from languages, dialects and staying abreast of the news to learning skills like picking locks, safe cracking, picking pockets and hacking into databases for information. She'd learned skills most parents didn't teach their children or warned their children to avoid.

Jasmine had earned her physical capabilities from her father. As an only child, she'd been the son her father never had. As an elite Sayeret Matkal, her father had kept his body in top condition. Jasmine had worked out at home with him and matched his running pace, determined to keep up with the father she loved so fiercely.

He'd taught her how to use a variety of weapons and the art of defending herself when she had no weapons at all. Because of her dedication to conditioning, her hand-to-hand combat skills and her ability to speak multiple languages, when she'd joined the Israeli military, she'd been accepted into Sayeret Matkal training soon after.

After the Athens affair and her subsequent release from the elite forces, she'd continued her training.

Now, due to circumstances out of her immediate control, she was on the verge of stealing from a museum the priceless copper scroll the Jordanians were so proud of.

Her jaw hardened. If she had to steal every last item in the museum, she would—anything to get Eli back alive.

She pulled the file from her satchel, glanced toward the room's entrance and then bent to stick the file into the little keyed lock. She fiddled with the lock until she tripped the mechanism, and the lock clicked open.

Jasmine tested the case top by lifting it several inches and then easing it back down. One down, several more to go. She'd work them a few at a time. When she had all the locks disengaged, she'd take the scroll and walk out of the museum or leave with the Jordanian film crew.

She cringed at the thought of waiting for the crew to head home. They could be there well into the night, filming take after take until they perfected the sequences.

No, she'd head out as soon as she could. She had a deadline she would not miss—could not miss—if she wanted to see Eli again.

Jasmine jimmied the locks on a few more of the displays and then returned to where the crew was staging the next scene with Sadie McClain.

In the shadow of a statue, one of Sadie's bodyguards shifted, his eyes narrowing. He wore a baseball cap, making it difficult to see his face.

Something about the way he held himself, the line of his jaw and the dark stubble on his chin struck a chord of memory in Jasmine. A shiver of awareness washed over her. She hurried past him without making eye contact.

When she looked back, the space where he'd been standing was empty.

Jasmine shook off a feeling of déjà vu and stood near the Jordanian camera crew, interpreting when needed but basically remaining quiet and out of the way.

With the preparations for the big scene complete, the camera crews stood ready for the director to shout *action*.

All other personnel were to move out of the line of sight of the cameras. This gave Jasmine the opportunity to slip back into the room with the copper scroll. When she heard the director shout, *"Action,"* Jasmine went to work quickly and efficiently, lifting the tops off the glass cases one at a time, wrapping each piece of the copper scroll in a soft swatch of fabric she'd brought in her satchel, handling them carefully so as not to break the fragile copper.

Jasmine placed each piece inside a box she'd designed specifically for transporting the delicate scroll. Once all the pieces were stored, she closed the box and slid it into her satchel.

Taking the extra time, she returned all the tops of the glass cases to their original positions so they wouldn't draw attention until a museum employee just happened to notice the cases were empty. That should buy her time to get the items out of the museum and out of Jordan before anyone became suspicious.

With her satchel tucked against her side, Jasmine hurried out of the room. At that moment, the director yelled, "Cut!" He motioned to the film crews and gave orders to the American and Jordanian cameramen.

Some of the Jordanians looked around for their interpreter.

Ready to get the hell out of the museum, Jasmine had no choice but to approach the cameramen and provide the necessary translation for the director. All the while, her hand rested on her satchel, anxiety mounting. The longer she stayed in the museum, the greater the chance of someone discovering the copper scroll was missing.

Short of racing out of the building and drawing

attention to herself, she remained, forcing a calm expression on her face when inside she was ready to scream. A life depended on her getting out of the museum and delivering the scroll—Eli's life.

ACE HAMMERSON—HAMMER back in his Navy days—thought he recognized the interpreter as soon as she'd stepped through the museum doors with the Jordanian camera crew. The more he studied her, the more he was convinced it was her.

Jasmine.

The woman with whom he'd spent an amazing week in Athens. A week he could never forget.

Had it really been four years?

Granted, she looked different from the last time he'd seen her. She'd changed. Her dark hair peeked out from beneath the black scarf she wore over her head and draped around her shoulders. Her curves were hidden beneath a long black tunic and black trousers. Her face was a little thinner, but those full, rosy lips and her eyes gave her away. There was no mistaking the moss green irises that had captivated him from the first time he'd met her at an outdoor café in the Monastiraki district of Athens.

He'd come to Antica Café on a recommendation from a buddy who'd been there a year earlier. The place had been packed, with no empty tables left. Tired and hungry after the twenty-hour journey from San Diego to Athens, he'd just wanted to eat, find his hotel and crash.

Rather than look for a less crowded café, he'd looked for an empty seat. A beautiful woman sat in a far corner, a book in her hand, enjoying a cup of expresso. Ace had approached, hoping she wouldn't blow him off, and asked if she spoke English.

She'd looked up at him with those amazing green eyes and smiled. In that moment, he'd felt a stirring combination of lust, longing and... strangely...home-coming wash over him. It could have been exhaustion, but more than hunger made him want to join this woman at her table.

She spoke English with a charming accent he couldn't place as either Greek or Arabic. When he'd asked if he could share her table, she'd tilted her head and stared at him with slightly narrowed eyes before finally agreeing with a relaxed smile.

That had been the beginning of the most incredible week of his life. His only regret was that he'd had to go back to work after that week. Before he'd had time to look her up, based on the phone number she'd given him, he'd deployed for several months to Afghanistan, where the mission had been so secret, they'd gone incommunicado to avoid any leaks.

By the time he'd returned to his home base, her number had been disconnected.

He hadn't known where to begin looking for her. In all their conversations, she'd barely revealed much about her life other than both her parents were dead, having been killed in a Hamas strike in Israel.

Because of her reference to her parents being killed in a Hamas strike, he'd assumed she was from Israel. She'd talked about her mother having been from Greece and her father from Israel. Like him, her father had been on vacation in Athens when he'd met her.

Ace had searched for her online, hoping to find out something about her whereabouts, but failed miserably. On his next vacation, he'd gone back to Greece, to the same restaurant where they'd met, hoping by some strange coincidence he'd find her there. He'd walked the same paths they'd walked through the city, looking for her. He'd stayed in the same hotel where they'd stayed, even insisting on the same room.

She hadn't been there. He'd gone to Tel Aviv and talked with some acquaintances he'd met during joint training exercises with the Israeli military. They hadn't heard of her.

As many people as there were in Israel, Ace hadn't expected to find her just by asking around. But he'd hoped that the same magic that had brought them together the first time would help him find her again. After a year, he'd admitted defeat and tried to forget her.

That had never happened. Every woman he'd dated after Jasmine had never sparked in him the fire and desire he'd felt with the woman he'd met in Athens.

Now, here he was, freshly out of the military, working with Hank Patterson and his team of Brotherhood Protectors in Amman, Jordan. Nowhere near Athens and four years after that fated affair, she walked back into his life.

New to the Brotherhood Protectors, Ace had agreed to accompany Hank and members of his team to Jordan to provide security for the film crew and actors who were friends of Hank's wife, Sadie McClain, on her latest movie set. He'd be an extra, there to observe one of the team's assignments.

They didn't always provide security for film crews, but since significant unrest existed in the countries surrounding the relatively stable Jordan, the film producers and studio had budgeted for a staff of security specialists.

Hank had worked with the studio and cut them a deal to ensure his people provided security for his wife and the crew there to make movie magic. Brotherhood Protectors were the most qualified to provide the safety net they might need if fighting spilled over the borders from countries surrounding Jordan.

Though he'd been excited and curious about the mechanics of making a movie, Ace's attention had shifted the moment Jasmine entered the museum.

His gaze followed her as she moved among the Jordanian film crew, standing between Americans and Jordanians, interpreting instructions when needed.

As the camera crew set up, Jasmine left them to wander around the museum, looking at ancient artifacts on display. At one point, she disappeared into a side room and remained gone for several minutes.

Ace started to follow when Hank approached him. "It's amazing, isn't it?"

Ace nodded. "Yes, sir."

Hank grinned. "I never imagined the amount of people it takes to produce a film until I accompanied Sadie on set for the first time."

Though Ace would rather focus his attention on Jasmine's movements, he gave his new boss all his attention. "I never realized there was so much involved."

"Right? It takes an incredible amount of coordination to set up a gig like this, from securing a location to getting permission, in this case, from the government to film here, to transporting all the equipment. Not to mention hiring people to do all aspects, including lighting, sound, video, makeup and costumes."

Ace's gaze remained on the door through which Jasmine had disappeared. "And that's just the filming," he commented, mentally counting the seconds Jasmine was out of his sight.

Then, she emerged from the room and rejoined her camera crew.

Ace let go of the breath he'd been holding.

Hank continued the conversation Ace had lost track of. "After the filming, there's the editing, music, marketing and more." The former Navy SEAL shook his head, his lips forming a wry smile. "I have so much more respect for all those names that scroll across the screen in the movie theater when they show the credits." He chuckled. "I always wondered, and now I know, what a key grip is."

Jasmine worked with the cameramen once more, then stepped back into the shadows.

Once the cameramen were in place, the lighting guy gave a thumbs-up. The director nodded, spoke with Sadie and then stepped back.

"They're about to start filming," Hank said.

When the director raised a hand, everyone grew quiet.

The director looked around at the placement of the cameras, Sadie and the lighting, then nodded.

Ace felt as though everyone took a collective breath, waiting for it...

"Action!" the director called out.

Ace's attention was divided between Jasmine, the actors, the cameramen and the supporting staff.

The beautiful, blond actress, Sadie McClain, did not command his attention like Jasmine.

Sure, Sadie was gorgeous, dressed in khaki slacks that hugged her hips, boots up to her knees and a flowing white blouse tucked into the narrow waist-band of her trousers.

Her mane of golden hair had been styled into a natural wind-swept look with loose waves falling to her shoulders. She worked her way through the museum corridor, pretending to be a patron until she arrived at a golden statue encased in a glass box.

As Sadie studied the statue, her character assessing her chances of stealing it, Jasmine slipped out of the main museum corridor into the side room again.

What was she doing in there?

Ace wanted to follow her, but to do so, he'd have to pick his way through the camera crews and lighting people. He didn't want to get in the way while the cameras were rolling. God forbid he should trip over a cable, make a noise or cast a shadow and make them have to start all over again.

So, he stood as still as a rock, all his attention on that room, counting the seconds until Jasmine came out or the director called, "Cut!"

Finally, Jasmine emerged from the room.

At the same time, the director yelled, "Cut!"

The crossbody satchel she'd worn pushed behind her now rested against the front of her hip; her hand balanced on it. Her head turned toward the museum entrance and back to the organized chaos of camera crews shifting positions and responding to the director's suggestions. An American cameraman approached the Jordanian crew and spoke in English.

Members of the Jordanian camera crew frowned, looking lost. One of them spotted Jasmine and waved her over.

Jasmine's brow furrowed. Her gaze darted toward the museum entrance once more before she strode across the floor to join the cameramen. She listened to the American cameraman and translated what he was saying for the Jordanians, who, in turn, grinned, nodded, and went to work adjusting angles.

Jasmine stepped back into the shadows.

Ace nodded to Hank. "Excuse me. I want to check on something."

Hank's eyes narrowed as his gaze swept through the people milling about. "Anything to be concerned about?"

Was there anything to be concerned about? Ace's gut told him something was off, but he didn't see a need to alarm Hank until he had a better idea of what. "No, I just want to look at some of the displays."

"Are you a history buff?" Hank asked.

"A little. I'm always amazed at artifacts that were created centuries much earlier than our country's inception."

Hank nodded. "Yeah, some of the items in this museum date back hundreds of years before Christ."

He gave Ace a chin lift. "Explore while you can. It looks like they're getting ready for another take."

His gaze remained on Jasmine as Ace strode across the smooth stone floors to the room Jasmine had visited twice in less than an hour.

The room was climate-controlled, with soft lighting and several display cases positioned at its center. At a brief glance, nothing appeared out of place, but as Ace moved closer to the display cases, he frowned. They appeared...

Empty.

His pulse leaped as he read the information plaque beside the row of cases.

Copper scroll. 1st century AD.

He circled the cases and found that they all had keyed locks. He didn't dare lift the tops off the cases. If he did, he'd leave his fingerprints all over the glass and possibly be accused of stealing what had been inside.

His stomach knotted. Jasmine had been in here. Had she come to steal the copper scroll? Did she have it stashed in that satchel she'd carried around all afternoon?

Ace spun on his heels and left the room. His gaze went to the last place he'd seen Jasmine. She wasn't there.

His pulse slammed into hyperdrive as he scanned the vast corridor where the film crew worked.

She was nowhere to be seen.

Ace strode toward the museum's entrance. As he neared the massive doors, someone opened the door and slipped through it.

That someone was Jasmine.

What the hell was she up to? If she'd stolen the scroll, he had to get it back. If he didn't, the museum would hold Hank's team responsible for the theft, especially considering they were the security team.

The copper scroll was a national treasure. If he didn't get it back, it could cause an international incident as well as delay film production.

Ace slipped out of the museum and paused to locate the thief.

Dark hair flashed as Jasmine rounded the corner of a building across the street from the museum.

Ace had to wait for a delivery truck to pass in front of him before he could cross the road. As he waited, two large men dressed in black entered the side street, heading in the same direction as Jasmine.

Once the delivery truck passed, Ace crossed the street and broke into a jog, hurrying toward the street Jasmine had turned onto.

As Ace reached the corner of the building, he heard a woman shout, "No!"

He turned onto the street.

A block away, the two men in black had Jasmine by her arms. She fought like a wildcat, kicking, twisting, and struggling while holding onto the satchel looped over her neck and shoulder. One man ripped the scarf from her head and reached for the satchel's strap.

"Hey!" Ace yelled, racing toward the men.

Jasmine used the distraction to twist and kick the man on her right in the groin. When he doubled over, she brought her knee up, slamming it into his face.

The injured man released her arm.

Jasmine turned to the other man, but not soon enough. He backhanded her on the side of her face hard enough to send her flying.

As she fell backward, the man grabbed the satchel and yanked, pulling it over her head as she fell hard against the wall of a building.

Clutching the satchel like a football, the man ran. His partner staggered to his feet and followed.

Ace would have gone after them but was more concerned about Jasmine.

The men ran to the end of the street. A car pulled up, they dove in, and, in seconds, they were gone.

Jasmine lay against the wall, her eyes closed, a red mark on her cheek where the man had hit her.

Anger burned in Ace's gut. He wanted to go after the men and beat the shit out of them. But he couldn't leave this injured woman lying in the street.

He knelt beside her and touched her shoulder. "Jasmine."

Jasmine moaned, blinked her eyes open and stared up into his face, her brow furrowing. "Ace?

What—" She glanced around, her frown deepening. "Where am I?" She met his gaze again. "Is it really you?"

His lips turned up on the corners. "Yes, it's me. You're in Jordan." His brow dipped. "You were attacked."

She pinched the bridge of her nose. "What happened?"

"Two men attacked you," he said.

"Two men..." She shook her head slowly. "Jordan..." Then her eyes widened, and she looked around frantically. "My satchel! Where is my satchel?"

"The men who hurt you took it."

She struggled to get to her feet. "Where did they go? I have to get it back." As she stood, she swayed.

Ace slipped an arm around her narrow waist. "They're gone."

"No!" She raked a hand through her hair. "I need that satchel." Jasmine pushed away from Ace and started running back the way they'd come, then stopped and looked over her shoulder. "Which way did they go?"

He tipped his head in the direction the men had gone.

When Jasmine turned in that direction, Ace stepped in front of her and gripped her arms. "They're gone. You won't catch up to them now."

"Why didn't you stop them? They stole my satchel!" She tried to shake off his grip on her arms.

His lips pressed together, and his grip tightened. "What was in the satchel, Jasmine?"

"Something important. I have to get it back. Please, let go of me."

"Was the copper scroll in your bag?" he asked quietly so only she could hear his words.

Her gaze locked with his. For a moment, she hesitated, as if deciding whether or not to trust him. Then she nodded. "I had to take it. If I don't get it back, someone I care about will die."

ABOUT THE AUTHOR

ELLE JAMES also writing as MYLA JACKSON is a *New York Times* and *USA Today* Bestselling author of books including cowboys, intrigues and paranormal adventures that keep her readers on the edges of their seats. When she's not at her computer, she's traveling, snow skiing, boating, or riding her ATV, dreaming up new stories. Learn more about Elle James at www.ellejames.com

Website | Facebook | Twitter | GoodReads | Newsletter | BookBub | Amazon

Or visit her alter ego Myla Jackson at mylajackson.com
Website | Facebook | Twitter | Newsletter

Follow Me!
www.ellejames.com
ellejamesauthor@gmail.com

ALSO BY ELLE JAMES

Gerard (#2)

Lucas (#3)

Beau (#4)

Rafael (#5)

Valentin (#6)

Landry (#7)

Simon (#8)

Maurice (#9)

Jacques (#10)

Brotherhood Protectors Yellowstone

Saving Kyla (#1)

Saving Chelsea (#2)

Saving Amanda (#3)

Saving Liliana (#4)

Saving Breely (#5)

Saving Savvie (#6)

Saving Jenna (#7)

Saving Peyton (#8)

Saving Londyn (#9)

Brotherhood Protectors Colorado

SEAL Salvation (#1)

Rocky Mountain Rescue (#2)

Ranger Redemption (#3)

Tactical Takeover (#4)

Colorado Conspiracy (#5)

Rocky Mountain Madness (#6)

Free Fall (#7)

Colorado Cold Case (#8)

Fool's Folly (#9)

Colorado Free Rein (#10)

Rocky Mountain Venom (#11)

High Country Hero (#12)

Brotherhood Protectors

Montana SEAL (#1)

Bride Protector SEAL (#2)

Montana D-Force (#3)

Cowboy D-Force (#4)

Montana Ranger (#5)

Montana Dog Soldier (#6)

Montana SEAL Daddy (#7)

Montana Ranger's Wedding Vow (#8)

Montana SEAL Undercover Daddy (#9)

Cape Cod SEAL Rescue (#10)

Montana SEAL Friendly Fire (#11)

Montana SEAL's Mail-Order Bride (#12)

Delta Force Strong

Ivy's Delta (Delta Force 3 Crossover)

Breaking Silence (#1)

Breaking Rules (#2)

Breaking Away (#3)

Breaking Free (#4)

Breaking Hearts (#5)

Breaking Ties (#6)

Breaking Point (#7)

Breaking Dawn (#8)

Breaking Promises (#9)

Hearts & Heroes Series

Wyatt's War (#1)

Mack's Witness (#2)

Ronin's Return (#3)

Sam's Surrender (#4)

Hellfire Series

Hellfire, Texas (#1)

Justice Burning (#2)

Smoldering Desire (#3)

Hellfire in High Heels (#4)

Playing With Fire (#5)

First Responder (#5)

Cowboys (#6)

Silver Soldiers (#7)

Secret Identities (#8)

Warrior's Conquest

Enslaved by the Viking Short Story

Conquests

Smokin' Hot Firemen

Protecting the Colton Bride

Protecting the Colton Bride & Colton's Cowboy Code

Heir to Murder

Secret Service Rescue

High Octane Heroes

Haunted

Engaged with the Boss

Cowboy Brigade

An Unexpected Clue

Under Suspicion, With Child

Texas-Size Secrets

Made in the USA
Monee, IL
12 July 2024